WEE MACGREEGOR

WEE MACGREEGOR

[*Frontispiece*

WEE MACGREEGOR

BY

J. J. BELL

With an Introduction by the Author, telling the story of the Book

THE MORAY PRESS
EDINBURGH AND LONDON

TO

JAMES WILLOCK

New Library Edition 1933
New Edition, reset, 1945
Reprinted 1946

EDINBURGH: THE MORAY PRESS, 57 GEORGE STREET
LONDON: 21 GREAT JAMES STREET, BEDFORD ROW, W.C.1

Printed in Great Britain by Neill & Co. Ltd., Edinburgh

INTRODUCTION

THE STORY OF THE BOOK

EVERY book, even the least important, holds a story not printed on its pages. It may be an interesting and illuminating story, worth telling for its own sake, though generally, we may suppose, it could matter only to the author and those who care for him.

The story of the present little book has a certain oddity, but that alone would be a far from sufficient reason for its appearing in print; and I should say at once that I am setting it down mainly because, when my friend, Robert D. Macleod, suggested my doing so, I saw an opportunity to record my acknowledgments, as I had often wished to do, to certain friendships, without which there could have been nothing to make a story about. In a way, it must be a fine thing for an author to be able to hold up his book and say: "Alone I did it!" Yet I reckon myself as more to be envied, with my memories of those who helped me, or made it possible for me, to do it.

.   .   .   .

Imagine, then, if you please, the case of a young man who, in the midst of a Science course at the University, took, as it were, the wrong turning, and with no literary equipment, save pen, ink, paper, some postage stamps and a little imagination, determined to become an author.

At the beginning of a new century, after five years of industry, his achievements amount to some hundreds of pieces of light verse scattered—many of them freely, in both senses of the word—among several dozens of periodicals; two little books of nursery rhymes, some scores of short stories, mostly in Scottish journals; two years' experience as sub-editor and book-keeper on a Glasgow illustrated weekly, and the privilege of filling a column, once a week, in the *Glasgow Evening Times*.

The last is his stand-by, and sometimes he feels that it is his limit. His parents kindly conceal, as they suppose, their doubts; his brothers and sisters admire everything he writes—which, of course, is very bad for him; his older relatives, having picked up the phrase somewhere, murmur "How precarious!"—and feel the better, no doubt, for having so delivered themselves. Still, he goes on, ever seeking, in particular, to improve his "English." Swinburne for verse and Anthony Hope for dialogue are among his models. . . . But you never can tell.

     .   .   .   .   .   .

My connection with the *Evening Times* began in this way. In those earlier years I had been writing short stories for one of its associated papers, the *Glasgow Weekly Herald*, and then, one day, the Editor of the latter, Mr A. Dewar Willock, invited me to come to his office. I had never beheld an Editor, nor had anybody I knew done so, and it is no exaggeration to say that I entered his room in an extremely highly strung condition. I was received by a young man, Mr George C. Porteous, then sub-editor—afterwards Editor—who did something to mitigate the strain till his chief appeared, a dark, bearded man, with the kindliest of eyes behind glasses, a humorist in the finest sense. He talked about my work and advised me where to send certain stories which had not been suitable for his journal—advice which I took, with fortunate results.

After that I called on him occasionally, without invitation; yet my self-confidence was not such that I could have introduced myself to any other editor.

One night I wrote a small poem. None of those early efforts have been preserved, but I have a vague recollection that it dealt with Spring, a Girl and, possibly, some Daffodils, or, maybe, a Dicky-bird. That does not suggest material for a sober newspaper, but in a daft moment I sent it to Mr Willock, asking whether he thought it would be of any use to the *Evening Times*, Two nights later my brother pointed it out—not without embarrassment, the thing being so sentimental—on the editorial page of that paper, whose circulation, within the next hour, I increased by six copies— why, I do not know, since they lay in my cupboard till long after.

On my next visit to Mr Willock he took me to another room, and kindly introduced me to Mr Michael Graham, thereby opening the door to a fairly long and entirely happy association with the *Evening Times*. For a year or so my contributions were confined to verse, and then, greatly daring, I sent in about half a column of prose. I have never, I am sorry to say, kept a diary, but trivialities may become landmarks in our lives, and I can still see myself writing those light paragraphs about Glasgow on a "Fair Saturday," and labelling them: "A Young Man's Fancies," not, of course, dreaming that here was the beginning of a long series of articles and sketches under that heading.

I have heard brother-writers remark that the older one grows the harder it is to come by fresh ideas, and I can well believe that it may be so where one's writing is confined to a certain subject, or subjects. But ought it to be so with the general journalist and the imaginative writer? Is there no inspiration in experience? As the old Devon saying has it:

> *A woman, a spaniel, a walnut-tree—*
> *The more you beat 'em, the better they'll be.*

I would except at least the spaniel, and insert the mature brain, which, I am assured by a man of science, will respond to almost any amount of flogging, provided the blood be in fair condition. In other words, the thing we importantly call mental exhaustion is really physical. At all events, this brings me to my point—namely, that with all the advantages of youth and its energy, and with all the world to choose from, there were occasions when I got "stuck"—and "stuck" far more badly than in later years—for an idea on which to build my article, or sketch, for the next Friday's

Evening Times, which I usually wrote on the Saturday, revised on the Monday, and delivered on the Tuesday.

Pardon, please, another triviality. Came a Saturday, when I felt I was going to be beaten. The family was from home for the week-end. Late in the day I left my own corner and came down to my father's library. A last resort —something serious. There was an early edition of *Hakluyt's Voyages* in beautiful binding, and I took down a volume.

I should be glad if a friendly psychologist would inform me as to the association of ideas between anything in Hakluyt and a working man, with his wife, baby and small boy, in Argyle Street, on a Saturday afternoon. The only lead I can give him is this. Ten years earlier, on board a Firth of Clyde excursion steamer, on a Glasgow "Fair Saturday," I had heard a distracted mother of five address her eldest in these words: "Macgreegor, tak' yer paw's haun', or ye'll get nae carvies to yer tea!"

Anyway, on a page of Hakluyt, I "saw" the little family, and that was the beginning. It was necessary, of course, to employ the vernacular, which I had done only once before, in a very short and rather sentimental sketch of a young working man and his wife inspecting a showcase of wondrous jewels in the Glasgow Exhibition of 1901.

I am well aware that I have been suspected of eavesdropping on tramway cars and elsewhere, and of furtively lurking in close-mouths, and in sundry other places, in order to gain my knowledge, such as it is, of the Glasgow, or Lowland, dialect; but the truth is that, just as I have never deliberately "studied" a fellow-creature, I had never made any effort to "learn" the speech of the people of the period. While I was familiar with the older men in my father's factory, who used the vernacular as a matter of course, I feel certain that I acquired little or nothing there. Indeed, I cannot doubt that from the lips of my paternal grandmother, a lady of the old school, who died when I was seven, fell all the quaint words and phrases—many of them embodied in nursery rhymes—into my memory, there to lie quiet till the years should bring a use for them.

So I sat down to write the first "Macgreegor" story, and, when it was finished, it struck me as pretty poor stuff. It certainly did not strike me as particularly funny—nor has "W.M." ever done that, while much of him has seemed to me rather pathetic. On the Monday it did not appear any brighter, but there was not time to try all over again, and at the last moment I sent it off to Mr Graham, with an apologetic note, and prepared myself for its rejection.

Yet, on the Friday afternoon there it was, in all the comfort and encouragement of print, though I still expected a letter, saying it had been allowed, for once, to pass, but must not happen again.

On the following Monday I went in to see Mr Willock, pretending that it was about another matter. Mr Willock laid one hand on my shoulder, gave me a hearty shake with the other, and said, in effect: "That's the stuff to give 'em, my boy! Do it again!" And presently Mr Graham said something almost as nice.

Any young writer who may do me the honour to read this will guess what that meant, and what the memory of those two men stands for in my life.

.   .   .   .

Letters from readers began to come to the office and direct to myself—kindly messages, though there was one, I recall, bitterly abusive, which, I confess, hurt me very much, though, no doubt, it was good for me.

The sketches did not appear in the *Evening Times* every Friday—Mr Graham and I saw the risk of overdoing it— but by the beginning of the following year I had accumulated fifteen or sixteen of them. Somebody—I am sorry I do not remember who it was—suggested collecting them into a cheap volume. I was going to be married in the autumn, and, while I had no illusions as to any rich reward, I thought it would be fun to have such a little book in being. However, it seemed that even the fun was to be denied me.

The publishers to whom, in turn, I submitted the material were quite unanimous. They generously admitted that the little sketches were amusing, but pointed out that their appeal was too local to justify the risk of publication. I offered the copyright to one firm for £10, to another for £5; but no, they were not tempted.

The idea of a book would have been dropped and forgotten had not I, by chance, mentioned it to my friend, J. A. Westwood Oliver, whose assistant I had been on the *Scots Pictorial*. He was, as always, sympathetic. He told me that his little company could not venture on the risks of book publication; then added that he thought *Macgreegor* might have a modest sale in Glasgow and the West, and that if I cared to guarantee £50, against possible loss, he would himself see it through the press. One of my brothers then sportingly offered to put up the £50.

There was so little material that the ordinary size of page had to be rejected, and we chose a format already made popular by Barry Pain's *Eliza*—6 by 3½ inches. I wanted the price to be sixpence, but deferred to Mr Oliver's theory that anyone who would rashly give the smaller coin for such a book would just as rashly part with the larger. The title was to be simply *Macgreegor*, and the early editions were printed with the solitary word at the top of the pages. At the last moment, however, as the cover was going to press, Mr Oliver suggested the addition of the "Wee," which, I cannot doubt, made a big difference in the popularity of the title.

Almost at the last moment, too, 'it was decided to have a picture on the cover. Some drawings were hurriedly obtained, but all were rather commonplace, if grotesque, representations of the conventional "bad boy," and it was through the good offices of Mr William Hodge, head of the printing firm, that we got the John Hassall drawing, which undoubtedly drew many an eye to the book. Then Mr Oliver gave an order for 3000 copies, though I had almost implored him to confine it to 2000.

And by now you will be agreeing that I had not very much to do with *Wee Macgreegor*.

.   .   .   .   .

I was married in October, and my wife and I went to

live in a quiet place on the Clyde, some five-and-twenty miles from the city. The book was published on 23rd November, and we wondered anxiously what was happening to it. A week passed; then came a telegram from Mr Oliver. The first printing was exhausted; a second was on the machines. By the end of the year the sales were 20,000.

The Press notices were extraordinarily generous. One in the *Glasgow Evening News*, by Neil Munro, whom, though he lived just across the water, I was not to meet till ten years later, must have been very helpful. Later, when the circulation had got to 50,000 or so, he wrote me a letter, threatening to come over with the family dirk. Another notice, by William Archer, in the *Morning Leader* was the book's best London introduction.

There was much pleasant correspondence from all parts of the world, even from remote corners, some from children, which was the pleasantest of all. Traders seemed to see a virtue in the title and the Hassall drawing, for presently appeared "Wee Macgreegor" lemonade, matches, china, "taiblet," picture postcards, sardines, and so forth. Sober-minded persons called it a "craze," and I should be the last to contradict them, for its favour from the English reader has always been inexplicable to me.

When the sales in this country had reached 60,000 news came over that the book was being "pirated" in America, where I had never thought of taking out copyright. The score or so of "pirated" editions were mostly cheap and crude productions. For some reason, best known to themselves, the publishers did not use the Hassall drawing; possibly they felt it was not "Scotch" enough. Most of them displayed effigies of little boys—in one instance, I believe, of a little girl—in full Highland costume, obviously copied from outfitters' catalogues. We had a copyright edition printed in Canada, but these American productions swamped it. Messrs Harper & Brothers, New York, published an "authorized edition," making a beautiful little book of it, and recognized myself in the matter, which was, of course, an act of grace on their part.

On this side, in 1903, Mr Oliver's company issued editions in cloth and leather, with illustrations by A. S. Boyd, but, naturally, the big demand was for the original little paper-covered volume. This is not the place for figures—though I have quoted some already—but, having heard so many extravagant estimates, I may take this opportunity of stating that the sales of the book in its original form did not pass the quarter-million. I do not suppose that many of those flimsy copies are in existence to-day. When Mr Oliver's company went out of business, the publishing of *Wee Macgreegor* was transferred to Messrs Mills & Boon, London, who by including its sequel made a sizable shilling book. For a time, too, it had considerable prosperity as one of *The Daily Mail* "Sixpennies." Then, in 1913, Messrs Thos. Nelson & Son took it into their remarkable series of "Sevenpennies," which, however, was checked by the rising costs of war-time, and later they put it into exceedingly neat forms, at 1s. 6d. and 2s., in which they have kept it alive ever since.

I must not neglect to say that in its first months the little thing was greatly helped by the proprietors and managers of the Glasgow railway station bookstalls, who not only displayed it most lavishly, but kept their boys shouting up and down the platforms, with copies. Some of those boys were wonderful young salesmen. They could sell the book to its author.

.   .   .   .   .

In 1911, Mr Alfred Wareing, Director of the Glasgow Repertory Theatre, conceived the idea of putting *Wee Macgreegor* on the stage, and in December presented a play, or rather series of episodes, adapted from the book. It was produced by Harold Chapin, the brilliant young playwright and fine soldier lost to us early in the War, and myself. The big difficulty at the outset was to find a boy to play the name part, and I still wonder what we should have done but for my friend, the late R. J. Maclennan, of the *Evening News* —the helping hand again, you see!—who took trouble to discover a likely lad for us. Willie Elliott, a messenger-boy, was fourteen, little for his age, nice-looking and intelligent. He had no ambition to become an actor, but the job, I suppose, seemed worth his while. It was my duty to take him through his part, and for a time he fairly baffled me by turning the vernacular into fairly good English. Eventually, thanks to the untiring patience of the chief producer and the principals, he did very well, being little troubled by self-consciousness. As far as I know, it was the only part he ever played. When the War came he enlisted in the Gordons, was three times wounded, and is now, I believe, raising a family in Canada. The play ran for seven weeks at the Royalty, and was afterwards taken on a short tour. As drama, it was without merit; its dialect alone would have prevented its going far afield; but the players made the most of it, and the author confesses that it did him good to hear the audience laugh.

Wee Macgreegor—as small boy—has not been screened. In the old "silent" days a contract for its filming was signed, and a sum was paid, but the producing company did not survive to make the picture. Nor has it been translated into any foreign language, though I have a record, dated 1904, of a gallant but misguided Frenchman who threw down the pen—and perhaps threw up the inkpot—about the middle of the second chapter. German philologists have written pleasant letters about some of the words, such as "toorie" and "peely-wally," but have shown no interest in the tale. Numerous persons wrote asking the meaning of "jaw-box." A gentleman in South Africa has, I believe, done a chapter or two into English, for use in schools. Two letters I particularly prize: one from a little girl in Ross-shire, who asks me to write "some more," tells me she is seven, and signs herself "Yours very truly"; the other from the grand-daughter of Dr Samuel Smiles, the famous author of *Self-Help*, who informs me that "the old gentleman" always carries a copy in his dressing-gown.

.   .   .   .

With the present edition, issued primarily to meet the need for a library size of the book, *Wee Macgreegor* is certainly in the handsomest dress he has had since he was born. Whether he deserves it is not for his author to say, more especially as his coming into the world and his continued (miraculous) existence therein have been—as has been shown—so largely due to sheer friendliness; none the less his author is grateful to the publishers, to whom the idea of the present edition belongs.

The earlier editions are dedicated to A. Dewar Willock and to Michael Graham, and to their Memories; and now I am happy to be allowed to dedicate this new edition, as seems right and fitting to do, to the son of the one and successor of the other—James Willock, Editor of the *Glasgow Evening Times*.

J. J. B.

ABERDEEN,
October 1933.

PUBLISHER'S NOTE

WITH the reissue of this edition of *Wee Macgreegor* it is appropriate that a short note be added by way of postscript. John Joy Bell's sudden passing, on 14th November 1934, in the midst of a busy and happy life, aroused as a first reaction, in the minds of those who loved him, a feeling akin to resentment. A man whose wholesome humour and utterly unselfish interest in life and work were such fine correctives to the prevailing paganism and vulgarity that characterize so much of modern entertainment had passed from us in his prime.

Perhaps it is good that it should have happened so, and we who knew him well will remember him as a man at his best: his quiet heroism in face of overwhelming difficulties, his genial camaraderie, his delightful sense of fun, and his generous understanding of the other fellow's point of view; all qualities beloved of the gods!

"It's no' that dear," said John thoughtfully.

"Weel, it's guid stuff. But I'm gey sweirt to pey sae muckle fur whit I can dae wi'oot. An' Macgreegor's needin' a new bunnet."

"His bunnet's fine. Jist you gang in, Lizzie, an' buy whit ye've got yer e'e on. We'll see aboot a bunnet efter. Dod! ye maun ha'e yer Ne'erday, wumman, like ither folk. Awa' wi' ye!"

"I'll tak' wee Jeannie in wi' me," said Lizzie, looking pleased. "I'm shair yer airm's sair wi' haudin' her. She's gettin' a big lassie—are ye no', ma doo?" She stepped into the doorway, but returned for a moment. "See an' keep a grup o' Macgreegor, John," she said.

"Oh, ay! Him an' me'll jist tak' a bit daunner up an' doon till ye come oot."

Having wiped from his face the sticky traces of his daughter's affection, and set his pipe going with several long breaths of satisfaction, he held out his hand to his son, with "Come on, Macgreegor."

Macgreegor slipped his small fist into the big one, and they set off slowly along the crowded pavements, stopping frequently to see the sights of the street and the windows, while the youngster asked innumerable questions, mostly unanswerable.

"Ha'e ye ett yer baurley sugar?" asked his father, during a pause in the childish queries.

"Ay; I've ett it. . . . It's no' as nice as taiblet, Paw."

"But ye'll no' be carin' fur taiblet noo?"

"Taiblet's awfu' guid," returned Macgreegor guardedly, with a glance upwards at his parent's face. "Wullie Thomson's paw gi'es him taiblet whiles."

"Aweel, Macgreegor, I'm no' gaun to *gi'e* ye taiblet. . . . But if ye wis pittin' yer haun' in ma pooch ye micht—— Ye're no' to let on to yer Maw, mind!"

The enraptured Macgreegor's hand was already busy, and a moment later his jaws were likewise.

"Ye've burst the poke, ye rogue," said John, feeling in his pocket. "Noo, ye're to get nae mair till the morn.

Yer Maw wud gi'e 't to me if she kent ye wis eatin' awmonds."

"I'll no' tell," said Macgregor generously.

As they approached the warehouse once more, John carefully wiped his son's mouth, and vainly endeavoured to assume an expression of innocence.

However, when Lizzie joined them she was too pleased and proud for the moment to suspect anything.

"Gi'e Jeannie to me," said John

"Na, na; I'll cairry her a wee. I got a sate in the shope. But I'll gi'e ye ma paircel. It'll maybe gang in yer poket."

"Jist," said her husband, as he stuffed in the long brown-paper package. "Did ye get whit ye wantit?"

"Ay, John, an' I bate them doon a shullin'."

"Ye're a rale clever wumman! Come, an' we'll gang an' see the waux-works."

"Paw," put in Macgreegor, "I wudna like to be a waux-work when I wis deid."

"Haud yer tongue, Macgreegor," said his mother. "John, ye maun check him when he says sic awfu' things."

"Aw, the wean's fine, Lizzie. . . . Macgreegor, ye're no' to say that again," he added, with an attempt at solemnity.

"Whit wey is folk made intil waux-works?" inquired his son, not greatly abashed.

"Oh, jist to amuse ither folk."

"But whit wey——" Macgregor's inquiry was interrupted by his colliding violently with a bag carried by a gentleman hurrying for his train.

"Ye see whit ye get fur no' lukin' whaur ye're gaun," said his mother. "Pit his bunnet stracht, John. . . . Puir mannie, it wis a gey sair dunt," she added gently.

"I'm no' greetin', Maw," said Macgregor, in a quavering voice, rubbing his eyes with his cuff.

"That's a brave lad!" said Lizzie.

"Never heed, Macgreegor! Ye'll be a man afore yer mither!" said John.

Thus consoled, the boy trotted on with his parents until they reached the gaudy entrance to the waxworks.

"Noo, I'll tak' Jeannie," said the husband.

"Ay; that'll be the best wey fur gaun in.   An' I'll tak' the paircel, fur it'll be in yer road."   So saying Lizzie handed her charge to John.   Then she pulled the parcel from his pocket; and lo and behold! it came out accompanied by sundry fragments of almond tablet, which fell on the pavement.

John would have dropped anything else but his present burden.   Macgregor gazed at the dainties at his feet, but did not dare attempt to secure them.   Lizzie looked pitilessly from one to the other.   It was a tableau worthy of wax.

But who can follow the workings of the childish mind? Two tears crept into Macgregor's eyes as he raised them fearfully to his mother's face.

"Paw never ett ony," he mumbled.

The expression on Lizzie's face changed to astonishment.

"Whit's that ye say?"

"P-p-paw never ett ony," the boy repeated.

And then, of a sudden, Lizzie's astonishment became amusement.

"Deed, ye're jist a pair o' weans!"   And she laughed against her will.

"It wis a' ma fau't, Lizzie," said John.

"Ay; ye sud ha'e pit the taiblet in yer ither poket!   Eh? . . . Na, na, Macgreegor, ye'll jist let the taiblet lie," she exclaimed, as the boy stooped to seize it.

"There nae glaur on it, Maw."

"Ay, but there is.   Come awa'!"

And away Macgregor was pulled to see the waxworks.

But why did Paw wink at his son and point stealthily to his "pooch"?

A VISIT TO THE ZOO

"Paw," said Macgregor, as the family party turned out of Sauchiehall Street into Cambridge Street, "Paw, whit wey dae they ca' it the Zoo?"

"Deed, Macgreegor, ye bate me there," returned Mr Robinson. "Lizzie," turning to his wife, "Macgreegor's speirin' whit wey they ca' it the Zoo."

"Macgreegor's aye speirin'," said Lizzie. "If they didna ca' it the Zoo, whit wud they ca' it?"

"Weel, that's true," observed her husband. "But it's a queer word, Zoo; an' the mair ye think o' 't, the queerer it gets. I mind I yinst——"

"Paw, wull we shin be there?" inquired his son, whose philological craving was apparently neither severe nor lasting.

"Ay, ye'll be there in a meenit. Lizzie, are ye shair it's a' richt aboot takin' wee Jeannie in to see the beasts? I doot she'll be frichtit."

"Frichtit? Nae fear, John! Wee Jeannie's no' that easy frichtit. Losh me! When the meenister wis in the hoose on Wensday, wee Jeannie wisna a bit feart—wis ye, ma doo? She jist laucht til him, an' played dab at his e'e wi' the leg o' her auld jumpin' jake. Mr Broon wis fair divertit an' gi'ed her yin o' his cough lozengers. Na, na, John; she's no' that easy frichtit."

"Aweel, ye ken best, Lizzie. See, gi'e her to me."

"Oh, I'll haud her till we get inside. She'll shin be walkin' her lanesome—wull ye no', honey? Jist keep a grup o' Macgreegor, John, or he'll be fleein' awa' an' gettin' tin ower or wannert."

"Paw," said Macgregor, "I see the Zoo."

"Ay, thon's it. Ye never seen wild beasts afore, Macgreegor."

"I near seen wild beasts in the shows at the Lairgs, Paw."

"Aw, ay; ye wis bidin' wi' yer Aunt Purdie then. She wud be feart to gang in whaur the beasts wis."

"Aunt Purdie's an auld footer," said Macgregor.

"Whisht, whisht!" interposed his mother. "Ye're no' to speak that wey aboot yer Aunt Purdie. She's a rale dacent wumman. . . . John, ye sudna lauch at Macgreegor's talk; ye jist mak' him think he's clever."

"Aw, the wean's fine, Lizzie. Weel, we'll get across the road noo."

"Whit wey——" began the boy.

"Macgreegor, tak' yer Paw's haun'. I'm no' wantin' ye to be catched wi' yin o' thae electric caurs," said his mother.

The street was crossed without mishap, and presently the quartet found themselves within the Zoo. For a couple of minutes, perhaps, they paused on the threshold, uncertain which direction to take. Then the announcement made by an official in a loud voice to the effect that a performance by the lions and tigers was about to take place on the west side of the building sent them hurrying thither with the crowd, Macgregor for once in his life being too overcome for speech.

Beyond sundry ejaculations, little conversation took place while the trainer exhibited his pluck and command over the brutes; and it might have been observed that Macgregor never once made the slightest attempt to withdraw his fingers from the fatherly clasp.

"Mercy me! It's maist wunnerfu'!" exclaimed Lizzie, when it was all over.

"Dod, it bates a'!" said John, as he took wee Jeannie from her arms.

And a small voice at his side whispered, "I wisna feart, Paw!"

"Macgreegor's sayin' he wisna feart, Lizzie," said John to his wife.

"Maybe he wisna," returned Lizzie, "but I can tell ye I

wis a' shakin' when thae muckle beasts wis loupin' aboot the man. I wis wunnerin' whit I wud dae wi' wee Jeannie if ony o' the beasts wun oot the cages an' commenced fur to pu' the heids an' legs aff the folk."

"Och, wumman, there nae fear o' that."

"If a beast wis comin' fur to pu' ma heid aff," remarked Macgregor, who had grown suddenly bold, "I—I—I wud—gi'e 't a kick!"

"Ye're the boy!" said his father.

"Ye sudna let him boast like that, John," said Lizzie reprovingly.

"Whit wud ye dae, Macgreegor," asked John, with a grin, "if a beast wis efter yer Maw?"

"I—I—wud pu' its tail," replied the valiant Macgregor. "And then I wud——" A loud roar from one of the lions interrupted him and caused him to clutch at his parent.

"Aw, Macgreegor," said his mother, "I doot ye wud jist rin awa' an' leave yer Maw to be ett."

The boy's lip trembled. "I wudna dae that, Maw," he said solemnly.

"Wud ye no', ma dearie?" said Lizzie, her voice softening. "Weel, weel, we'll say nae mair aboot it. Whit's yer Paw an' wee Jeannie efter noo?"

"It's an ephelant, Maw," said Macgregor, as they overtook the father and daughter, who were admiring the stuffed carcase of a huge elephant.

"He's no leevin'," John explained. "He's the yin that had to be shot a while syne."

"Whit wey wis he shot, Paw?"

"He was dangerous."

"Whit wey wis he dangerous?"

"I'm no' jist shair, but a man yinst tell't me the beast wis trampin' on his keepers, an' eatin' the bunnets aff the folk's heids."

"Paw, whit's thon big white oossie beast?"

"Thon yin? Dae ye ken, Lizzie?"

"I've seen picturs like it, John. It's a—oh, ay, it's a Polish bear."

"Dod, ay! It wud gey shin polish aff you an' me, wumman," said John, laughing heartily.

"Dod, ay!" echoed Macgregor.

"Ye're no' to say that," said Lizzie.

"Whit, Maw?"

"Ye're no' to say 'dod.'"

"Paw says it, Maw."

"Weel, yer Paw sudna say it."

"Whit wey, Maw?"

"Ha'e, Lizzie," said John, handing his wife a catalogue which he had just purchased, "that'll tell ye the names o' the beasts. Whit dae they ca' thon strippit——"

"Maw, whit's the name o' thon spotit yin?" cried Macgregor.

"They're baith Hyaenies," replied Lizzie, after consulting the numbers on the cages and the booklet. "Thon big black beast wi' the awfu' tae-nails is the Aswail or Sloth Bear."

"Ay, it's jist Aswail it's in its cage," remarked her husband with a chuckle.

"My! ye're rale smairt the day, John, wi' yer bit jokes. But whaur's Macgreegor?"

The youngster was discovered, after some search, at the other side of the building, gazing with an expression of awe at a couple of camels.

"Paw, the wee yin's face is unco like Aunt Purdie," he observed.

His father guffawed.

His mother frowned. "John, I've tell't ye afore no' to lauch when Macgreegor says impiddent things. I wunner at ye!"

"But, Lizzie, I cudna help it this time. Dod, I thocht it wis gey like yer brither's guidwife masel'!"

"John!"

"As shair's daith! It's jist the face she pits on when she's comin' oot the kirk on a wat Sawbath."

"Weel, she canna help her face, puir thing!" said Lizzie.

"I never cud unnerstaun' hoo yer brither Rubbert cud mairry sic an auld bogle, an' him wi' sic a braw sister."

"Hoots, John! Ye're fair aff at the nail the day!" said Lizzie, trying not to smile.

"Paw, whit wey ha'e the caymels nae trunks like the ephelants?"

"Macgreegor," remarked Lizzie, "ye wud turn Solyman hissel' dementit! Jist luk at the humphs on their backs, an' dinna fash yer——"

"Paw, whit wey ha'e the caymels got humphs?"

"Man, ye're a fair divert, Macgreegor!" said John. "Maybe it's because they ha'e nae trunks. See, there a penny fur ye. Awa' to the stall ower thonder, an' get a wheen biscuits fur the beasts."

"I'm gaun to feed the ephelants," Macgregor announced on his return.

"That's richt! See, there the big yin haudin' oot his trunk. . . . Dod, a biscuit's naethin' to him. Gi'e yin to wee Jeannie an' she'll feed the ither yin."

"Is the ephelant's trunk jist the same as a man's neb, Paw?" inquired Macgregor.

"Ay, jist the same."

"Whit wey dae folk no' pick up things wi' their nebs, Paw?"

"Aw, haud yer tongue, Macgreegor," said his mother. "John, bring wee Jeannie ower to see the paurrits."

The birds having been duly admired and commented upon, Macgregor was again discovered to be missing. This time he was found engaged in making faces at a family of monkeys.

"Come awa' frae the nesty things!" cried Lizzie. "I canna thole monkeys, John. Whit'll thon beast be in the watter?"

"The number's wan-twinty-nine."

"Oh, ay. Common Seal, frae the German Ocean. Ah, but that'll be the wee yin. The big yin's a Californian Sea Lion. Macgreegor, here a sea lion!"

"It's no vera like a lion, Maw. . . . I see its whuskers! Whit wey has it got nae ooss on its feet?"

"Thae things isna feet. Thae's fins."

"Whit wey has it nae ooss on its fins, Paw?"

"Maybe it cudna soom wi' ooss on its fins."

"Whit wey cud it no' soom wi' ooss on——"

"Come awa' an' see this extraornar' beast, Macgreegor," said Lizzie. "The book says it's ca'ed a tapir."

"Whit wey is't ca'ed a tapir, Maw?"

"Gi'e 't a bit biscuit," returned his mother evasively. "Puir beastie, it's lukin' gey doon i' the mooth, is't no', John?"

"It's a' that. But I wud be doon i' the mooth, masel', Lizzie, wi' a neb like that on me. See an' no' let it nip yer fingers, Macgreegor."

"Whit wey is its neb sae shoogly, Paw?"

"Dod, Macgreegor, I'm thinkin' it kens ye. It's wagglin' its neb at ye fur anither bit biscuit."

"John," said his wife, "I'll tak' wee Jeannie an' ha'e a sate fur a wee."

"Are ye wearit? Wud ye no' like a dish o' tea?"

"Och, I'm no' needin' tea, John."

"Plenty folk tak' tea when they're no' needin' it. Come on, Lizzie!"

Lizzie shook her head and muttered something about "gentry" and "wastry."

"I—I got a rise in ma pey the day, Lizzie," said her husband suddenly.

"Did ye that, John?"

"Ay! Hauf-a-croon."

"Deed, I wis thinkin' it was mair nor naethin' that wis makin' ye sae jokey-like," said Lizzie with a laugh.

"Come on, then, Lizzie. Here, Macgreegor!"

"Paw, whit wey——"

"Aw, ye'll see the beasts again in a wee while. Cud ye eat a pie?"

Macgregor drew a long breath. "Cud I no'?" he exclaimed, beaming.

III

AUNT PURDIE'S TEA-PARTY

THE Robinsons were on their way to take tea at Aunt Purdie's, and the anxious Lizzie was counselling her son regarding his behaviour at the table of that excellent lady.

"Noo, Macgreegor, ye're no' to affront me. Yer Aunt Purdie's rale genteel, an' awfu' easy offendit."

"Dod, ay!" said John, "ye'll ha'e to mind yer Q.P.'s the day, as the sayin' is."

"Dod, ay!" said Macgregor.

"I've tell't ye dizzens o' times, Macgreegor, ye're no' to say that," said his mother.

"I furgot, Maw."

"If yer Aunt Purdie wis hearin' ye speak that wey she wud be sair pit oot. An', John," turning to her husband, "ye sud be mair carefu' whit ye say afore the wean. He's jist like a paurrit fur pickin' up words."

"Dod, ay!" said John seriously, "I'll ha'e to be carefu', Lizzie."

"Ye're a terrible man," said his wife, frowning and smiling.

"Wull I get a tert at Aunt Purdie's?" inquired Macgregor.

"Ye'll see whit ye'll get when ye get it," replied his mother. "An' mind, Macgreegor, ye're no' to be askin' fur jelly till ye've ett twa bits o' breid an' butter. It's no mainners; an' yer Aunt Purdie's rale parteeclar. An' yer no' to dicht yer mooth wi' yer cuff—mind that. Ye're to tak' yer hanky an' let on ye're jist gi'ein' yer nose a bit wipe. An' ye're no' to scale yer tea nor sup the sugar, if ony's left in yer cup when ye're dune drinkin'. An' if ye drap yer piece on the floor, ye're no' to gang efter it; ye're jist to let on ye've ett it. An' ye're no'——"

28

"Deed, Lizzie," interposed her husband, "ye're the body to think aboot things!"

"Weel, John, if I dinna tell Macgreegor hoo to behave hissel', he'll affront me. It's maybe a sma' maitter to a man, John, but a wumman disna like to be pit oot afore her guid-sister. An', John, ye're to try an' be discreet yersel', an' think afore ye mak' a bit joke—fur she's a rale genteel wumman, an' awfu' easy offendit."

"But yer brither likes a lauch, Lizzie."

"Ay, Rubbert's a herty man; but a' the same, John, ye're no' to gar him lauch abin his breith. An' yer no' to lauch yersel' if Macgreegor tries to be smairt."

"A' richt, Lizzie," said her husband good-humouredly. "Dod, I'm thinkin' ye're jist aboot as feart fur me as fur the wean."

"Havers, John! I'm no' finnin' fau't wi' you. It's jist that ye whiles furget yer——"

"Ma Q.P.'s."

"Ay, yer Q.P.'s, as ye ca' it. I aye thocht Q.P.'s wis a kin' o' fit-ba'."

Her husband was about to explain when Macgregor exclaimed that Aunt Purdie's dwelling was in sight.

"Ay, it's the third close," remarked John, proceeding to plug his pipe with a scrap of newspaper. After that he pulled up his collar, tightened his tie, cocked his hat a little over one eye, winked at his wife, and chucked his little daughter under the chin.

"I wud just as shin be at hame, Lizzie," he observed, as they turned into the close.

"Whisht, John! Mrs Purdie's a rale dacent wumman, an'—an' we needna wait ower lang. See if ye can gi'e Macgreegor's hair a bit tosh up. It's awfu' ill to lie. . . . Noo, John, ye'll gang furrit an' ring the bell. Mind, ye're to speir if Mrs Purdie is in afore ye gang ower the doorstep."

"But she wudna ha'e askit us to wur tea if she had been fur gaun oot," said John.

"Tits, man! D'ye no' ken Mrs Purdie keeps a servant lass, an' ye maun speir at her if her mistress is in. Mind, yer no' to say 'it's a fine day,' or onythin' like that; ye're jist to speir if Mrs Purdie's in.   D'ye see?"

"Weel, weel, wumman, onythin' to please ye!" And John pulled the bell-handle.   "I ken she's in," he whispered. "I hear her roarin' at somebody."

"Sh! John.   Jist dae whit I tell't ye."

The door was opened and John bashfully repeated the formula.

"Will you please step in?" said the domestic, a small, rosy-cheeked girl, who still showed her ankles though she had put up her hair.

"Dicht yer feet, Macgreegor, dicht yer feet," said Lizzie in a quick, loud whisper.   "See, dicht them on the bass."

Macgregor obeyed with great vigour, and followed the others into the lobby.

"Paw, we've a brawer nock nor thon yin," he remarked in a husky undertone, pointing at a grandfather's clock in a corner.

"Whisht!" said his mother nervously.

"Wull I pit ma bunnet in ma pooch, Maw?" asked the boy.

"Na, na!   John, hing his bunnet up aside yer ain."

Just then Mrs Purdie appeared and bade them welcome; and presently they were gathered in the parlour, wherein the table was already laid for tea.   Mr Purdie was getting on well in the world—his grocery establishment was gaining new customers daily—and Mrs Purdie was inclined, alas! to look down on her homely relatives, and to regard their manners and speech as vulgar, with the sole result that her own manners were frequently affected, while her speech was sometimes a strange mixture.

"And how are you to-day, Macgregor?" she asked the boy as they sat round the fire.

"I'm fine," replied Macgregor, glancing at the good things on the table.

"Fine what?" said Aunt Purdie severely.

"Ye sud say, 'Fine, thenk ye,'" whispered his mother, giving him a nudge.

"Fine, thenk ye," said Macgregor obediently. "I wis at the Zoo yesterday."

"Oh, indeed! Was you? And what did you see at the Zoo?"

"Beasts, thenk ye," said Macgregor.

"An' hoo's Rubbert?" asked Lizzie with some haste.

"Robert is keeping well, thank you; but he's sorry he cannot leave the shope this evening. His young man was unfortunately rin over by an electric caur yesterday."

"Oh, thae caurs!" said Lizzie. "I'm aye feart fur Macgreegor gettin' catched, an' comin' hame wantin' a leg."

"Robert's young man got conclusion of the brain," said Aunt Purdie with great solemnity. "He was carrying a dizzen of eggs an' a pun' of the best ham when the melancholy accident occurred."

"Dae ye tell me that?" exclaimed Lizzie. "An' wis the eggs a' broke?"

"With two exceptions." And Aunt Purdie went on to describe the accident in detail to Lizzie, while John and Macgregor looked out of the window, and wee Jeannie, who had been put on the floor to "play herself," found amusement in pulling to pieces a half-knitted stocking which she discovered in a basket under the sofa.

Soon the little rosy-cheeked maid entered with the teapot, and they all took their places at table, wee Jeannie being lifted up on her mother's knee and warned not to touch the knife.

"Mr Robison," said Aunt Purdie, looking very hard at John, "kindly ask a blessing."

John turned red and mumbled something, at the end of which he wiped his brow and loudly blew his nose.

The hostess, after looking for a moment as if she thought it rather an inferior "blessing," commenced her hospitable duties.

"I'm no' wantin' a joog, Maw," said Macgregor to his mother, as he observed Aunt Purdie filling a mug with milk and hot water.

"It's fur wee Jeannie," whispered Lizzie. "But ye're jist to tak' whit ye get."

Conversation flagged for the first five minutes. Then Mrs Purdie broke the silence.

"Have you been going out much this winter, Mr Robison?" she inquired in her best style.

For an instant John gaped. "Dod, Mrs Purdie, I'm gled to say I've no' been aff ma work a day since the New Year."

"I mean out to entertainments, parties, and conversonies," said Mrs Purdie with a pitying smile.

"Oh, ay. Aweel, Lizzie, an' me likes the fireside, but we've been to the Zoo an' the pantymine an' twa-three surrees."

"I like surrees," observed Macgregor, digging into a pot of jam. By a strange mischance he had already dropped two pieces of plain bread and butter on the floor, but to his credit it must be recorded that he had remembered his mother's injunction not to attempt to recover them.

"Ay, Macgreegor's the yin fur surrees," said John. "He cam' hame frae the Sawbath-schule surree the ither nicht wi' fower orangers an' guid kens hoo mony pokes o' sweeties."

"Ay, an' he had to get ile i' the mornin'," said Lizzie, whose time was chiefly occupied in feeding wee Jeannie.

"Do you like oil?" said Mrs Purdie, smiling sourly at Macgregor.

"Naw," returned the boy, with his mouth full. "Dae you like ile, Aunt Purdie?"

"Whisht!" said his mother reprovingly.

"Assist yourself to a cookie, Mr Robison," said Mrs Purdie, a trifle confused. "And pass your cup. Mrs Robison, is your tea out?"

"Thenk ye," said Lizzie. "This is rale nice cake, Mrs Purdie."

"It was recommended to me by Mrs M'Cluny, the doctor's wife. Mrs M'Cluny is very highly connected, quite autocratic, in fact. Her and me is great friends. I expect to meet her at the Carmunnock conversonie on Monday night—a very select gathering. Her and me——"

"Paw, I want a tert."

"Na, John," said Lizzie, "he's had yin."

"I want anither, Maw."

"Ye canna get anither, Macgreegor. Weel, Mrs Purdie, ye was sayin'——"

"I was observing——"

"Paw, gi'e's a tert," said Macgregor in a whisper.

John winked at his son, and stealthily moved the dish of dainties in his direction.

The two ladies were discussing the coming "conversonie," and appeared oblivious to what was going on. The plate came nearer and nearer, and at last Macgregor's eager paw went cautiously towards it. The tart was secured, but as the boy drew back his hand his mother detected him.

"Macgreegor!" she exclaimed.

The hapless youngster started guiltily. Over went the jam-pot, spreading its contents on the cloth; over went Macgregor's teacup, to be smashed to atoms on the floor. Wee Jeannie, with a gurgle of delight, evidently under the impression that something in the way of entertainment was expected of her, tipped her mug after the cup, while her father, rising in confusion, sent a plate and five cookies to swell the wreckage.

John stood helpless; Lizzie sat speechless and pale; wee Jeannie, discovering that it wasn't a joke after all, set up a dismal wailing; and Macgregor, with quivering lip and misty eye, stared at the ruin he had wrought. No one dared to look at Aunt Purdie. Her expression was grim—very grim indeed. When she did speak, her words were few but incisive. They had reference to the bringing-up of children, of which, she thanked Providence, she had none. Poor Lizzie apologized for her son, expressed herself "fair affrontit" at his conduct, and declared that she would "sort" him when they got home.

The hour following tea was an uncomfortable one, and John did not conceal his relief at being out of the house.

c

"She'll no' ask us back," he observed.

Lizzie said nothing.

"Macgreegor's sayin' he's that sorry," said John presently.

"He'll be sorrier yet!" muttered Lizzie.

"He's saying he'll tak' ile if ye like," went on her husband.

"He'll get mair nor ile!"

"Aw, wumman, the wean cudna help it. It wis a' an accident. Let him aff this time, Lizzie. I broke a plate masel', ye ken, an' wee Jeannie broke a joog. Are we a' to get ile an'—an' the ither thing, dearie?" . . .

"Och, John, ye aye get ower me."

And so peace reigned again.

Ten minutes later John noticed that Macgregor was lagging behind. He went back a couple of steps and took his son's hand.

"Whit's that ye're pittin' in yer gab, Macgreegor?" he asked suddenly.

Cautiously Macgregor drew something from his pocket. "I'll gi'e ye a taste, Paw," he said generously. "It's a tert."

IV

"A DAUD O' POTTY"

"When I'm a man," observed Macgregor, leaning against the knees of his father, who was enjoying an evening pipe before the kitchen fire, "when I'm a man, I'm gaun to be a penter."

"A penter!" echoed John. "D'ye hear whit Macgreegor's sayin', Lizzie?" he inquired of his wife.

Lizzie moistened her finger and thumb, twirled the end of a thread, and inserted it into the eye of a needle ere she replied. "Whit kin' o' a penter? Is't pictur's ye're wantin' to pent, Macgreegor?"

"Naw!" said her son with great scorn. "I'm gaun to ha'e a big pot o' pent an' a big brush, an' I'm gaun to staun' on a ladder, an' pent wi' white pent, an' rid pent, an' bew pent, an'——"

"Aw, ye're gaun to be a hoose-penter, Macgreegor," said his father.

"Ay. But I'm gaun to pent shopes tae. An' I'm gaun to ha'e big dauds of potty fur stickin' in holes. I like potty. Here a bit!" And Macgregor produced from his trouser-pocket a lump of the greyish, plastic substance.

"Feech!" exclaimed Lizzie in disgust. "Whaur got ye that? Ye'll jist file yer claes wi' the nesty stuff."

"Wullie Thomson whiles gets potty frae his Paw. Wullie's Paw a jiner."

"I thocht you an' Wullie had cast oot," said John. "Ha'e ye been makin' freens wi' him again?"

"Naw. But I seen him wi' the potty, an' I askit him fur a daud."

"It wis rale nice o' the laddie to gi'e ye a bit," remarked Lizzie, looking up from her seam.

"He didna gi'e it, Maw. I tuk it frae him."

"Aw, Macgreegor!" said Lizzie, shaking her head reproachfully.

"Wullie's bigger nor me, Maw."

"Ay, but he's gey wake i' the legs."

"I hut him, an' he tum'lt; an' I jist tuk hauf his potty," said Macgregor unconcernedly.

John was about to laugh, when he caught his wife's eye.

"An' hoo wud ye like," she said, addressing her son, "if yer Paw gi'ed ye potty, an' anither laddie cam' an'——"

"Paw hasna ony potty."

John sniggered behind his hand.

"Weel," said Lizzie, casting her husband a severe look, and turning again to her son, "hoo wud ye like if yer Paw gi'ed ye taiblet, an' anither laddie cam' an' tuk hauf o' 't awa'?"

"I wud gi'e him yin on the neb twicet!" said Macgregor

boldly, going over to the window to see the lamps being lighted.

"But if he hut ye an' knockit ye doon?"

"I wudna let him. Paw hasna gi'ed me taiblet fur a lang while," said the boy over his shoulder.

"Macgreegor," said his mother solemnly, "I'm thinkin' ye're gettin' waur every day."

"Aw, the wean's fine, Lizzie," interposed John softly.

"Haud yer tongue, John," retorted Lizzie quietly. "The wean's no' fine! An' instead o' lauchin' at him, an' makin' a pet o' him, ye ocht to be gi'ein' him a guid skelpin'.'

"I've never skelpit a wean yet, an'——"

"It's easy seen ye've never skelpit Macgreegor, John. Ye jist let him get his ain wey, an' he disna ken when he's misbehavin' hissel'. Weans needs to be checkit whiles."

"Aweel, whit dae ye want me to dae, Lizzie?"

"I want ye to punish Macgreegor for hittin' that puir speldron o' a laddie Wullie Thomson, an' stealin' his potty," said Lizzie in an undertone.

Macgregor came back from the window with the putty plastered over his nose.

"Paw, see ma neb!" he said gaily, unaware of the conversation which had just passed concerning him.

John laughed loudly. "Dod, but ye've a braw neb the nicht, Macgreegor!"

"Tak' it aff this meenit!" cried Lizzie. "John, ye micht think shame o' yersel' to sit there lauchin' at his nesty tricks! D'ye no' mind hoo Mrs Cochrane's man tell't us his nose wis aye bew wi' him pittin' potty on't when he wis a wean? . . . Tak' it aff, Macgreegor, or I'll sort ye!"

Macgregor, but little abashed, returned to the window, removed the offending plaster, rolled it into a ball, and proceeded to squeeze it through his fingers with undisguised relish.

"John," whispered Lizzie, "dae whit I tell't ye."

"I canna," returned John miserably. "It micht wauken wee Jeannie," he added a little hopefully.

"I didna exac'ly say ye wis to—to whup the laddie," said his wife, "but ye maun gi'e him a lesson he'll no furget. I'm no' gaun to ha'e him boastin' an' ill-usin' ither weans. D'ye see?"

"But whit am I to dae, Lizzie?"

"I'll tell ye, John. Ye'll gang ower to the dresser an' open the wee drawer, an' ye'll tak' oot the taiblet ye brocht hame fur Macgreegor the morn—— Are ye listenin'?"

"Ay, wumman."

"An' ye'll tell Macgreegor ye bocht the taiblet fur his Setterday treat, thinkin' he deservit it, but ye've fun' oot he disna deserve it, an' ye canna gi'e him ony."

"Aw, Lizzie!"

"An' ye'll tie it up in a paircel, an' gar him tak' it to Wullie Thomson, an' gi'e it to Wullie Thomson, an' gi'e him back his potty furbye."

"Aw, Lizzie!"

"An' it'll be a lesson to Macgreegor no' to strike laddies waker nor hissel'. Ye wud be gey sair pit aboot, John, if a muckle laddie wis strikin' Macgreegor."

"Deed, wud I! But—but Macgreegor's that fond o' taiblet."

"Man, man, can ye no' think o' whit's guid fur Macgreegor? That's the wey ye spile him, John. Ye wud gi'e him the cock aff the steeple, if he cried fur't!"

"Maybe ye're richt, Lizzie. But it's a hard thing ye're askin'. Wud it no' dae to gi'e him hauf the taiblet to tak' to Wullie Thomson?"

"Na, na," said Lizzie firmly. "Here, Macgreegor," she called to her son. "Yer Paw wants to speak to ye. . . . Noo, John!"

With a huge sigh, John rose, went to the wee drawer in the dresser, and returned with the poke of "taiblet."

"Paw," said Macgreegor absently, "I like taiblet better nor potty."

The father glanced appealingly at the mother, but she was adamant. She had resumed her sewing, but was keeping an eye on the twain.

"Macgreegor," said John with a painful effort, "whit wey did ye strike puir Wullie Thomson?"

"I wantit a wee daud o' potty."

"Ay," murmured John, and paused for a moment. "Are ye sorry ye hut him?"

"Naw, I got the potty, Paw."

"But ye sud be sorry, Macgreegor."

"Whit wey, Paw?"

"Wis he greetin'?"

"Ay, wis he!"

John looked across at Lizzie for aid, but she was sewing diligently.

"Weel," he said haltingly, "yer Maw an' me arena vera pleased wi' whit ye done to Wullie Thomson. It wisna fair to strike the likes o' him."

Macgregor's visage began to assume an anxious expression'

"Yer Maw," continued John, "yer Maw says ye canna——"

"John!" murmured Lizzie warningly.

"Yer Maw and me thinks ye canna get ony taiblet the morn."

Macgregor's under lip shot out.

"An'—ye've got to gi'e the taiblet to Wullie Thomson, an' gi'e him back his potty furbye, an'—an'—oh, Lizzie, I canna say ony mair!"

It took a few seconds for the dire truth to dawn upon Macgregor, but when it did, a low wail issued from him, and the tears began to flow.

John was about to lift him upon his knee, but Lizzie interposed.

"Pit on yer bunnet, Macgreegor," she said quietly, "an' tak' the taiblet an' potty to Wullie Thomson. It's no' dark yet," she added, glancing out of the window.

"I'm no' wantin' to gi'e the taiblet to Wullie Thomson," sobbed the luckless youngster.

"Ye've jist to dae whit ye're tell't," returned his mother calmly, but not unkindly. "Ye're no' to be a tawpy noo," she went on, endeavouring to dry his eyes. "Ye're to be a man. Whit wud Wullie Thomson think if he seen ye greetin'? Eh, Macgreegor?"

Lizzie had struck the right note. The sobs ceased, though the breath still came gustily. He mopped the tears with his cap, and replaced it on his head.

"Am I to gi'e him a' the taiblet an' the potty furbye?" he inquired plaintively.

"Ay. An' ye're to say ye're sorry fur hurtin' him. He's no' a fine, strong laddie like yersel', Macgreegor—mind that! Yer Paw an' me wudna like if ye wis wake i' the legs like puir Wullie. Noo, jist gang an' gi'e him the taiblet an' his potty, an' see if ye canna mak' freens wi' him again."

"I'm no' wantin' to be freens," said Macgregor rebelliously. "I'm no' wantin' to gang."

"Are ye feart fur Wullie Thomson?" asked Lizzie. Another clever stroke!

"I'm no' feart! I'll gang!"

"Fine, man!" cried John, who had been listening in gloomy silence. "I kent ye wisna feart."

Macgregor began to feel himself rather a hero. In dignified silence he took the poke of "taiblet," which his mother had tied securely with a piece of tape from her work-bag, and departed on his errand.

John looked anxiously at Lizzie.

She sat down to her seam again, but her fingers were less deft than usual. They both eyed the clock frequently.

"He sudna be mair nor five meenits," remarked John. "I doot we wis ower hard on the wean, wumman."

Lizzie made no response, and ten minutes dragged slowly past.

"Did ye expec' he wud dae it?" asked John presently.

"Och, ay!" she answered with affected carelessness.

"I wisht I had went wi' him," said John.

Lizzie put in half-a-dozen stitches in silence. Then she said: "Ye micht gang an' see whit's keepin' him, John."

"I'll dae that, Lizzie. . . . Dae ye think I micht buy him

a bit taiblet when I'm ootbye?" He asked the question diffidently.

His wife looked up from her seam. "If ye like, John," she said gently. "I'm thinkin' the laddie's had his lesson noo. He's unco prood fur a wean, is he no'?"

"Ay," said John. "There no' mony like Macgreegor." He nodded to his wife, and went out.

About twenty minutes later father and son re-entered the house together. Both were beaming.

"I cudna get Macgreegor awa' frae Wullie Thomson, Lizzie," said John, smiling.

"Weel, weel," said his wife, looking pleased. "An' did ye gi'e Wullie the taiblet an' the potty, Macgreegor?"

"Ay, Maw."

Whereupon his mother caught and cuddled him. "Gi'e him a bit taiblet, John," she said.

John did so right gladly and generously, and Macgregor crumped away to his heart's content.

"An' whit kep' ye waitin' at Wullie's a' this time?" inquired Lizzie pleasantly.

"He gi'ed me a big daud o' potty, Maw," said the boy, producing a lump the size of an orange.

"Oh!" exclaimed Lizzie, trying not to look annoyed.

"An' him an' me ett the taiblet," added Macgregor.

V

ON ROTHESAY ESPLANADE

"Hech! Macgreegor, ye're gaun ower quick fur me," gasped Grandfather Purdie, as the youngster whose hand he held hurried him along the Rothesay Esplanade in the early afternoon sunshine.

"I cud gang quicker, Granpaw."

"Deed, ay! Ye're fine an' soople! But the boat'll no' be in fur mair nor hauf-an-'oor. Sae we'll jist tak' a sate fur a wee. I'm gettin' auld, Macgreegor, I'm gettin' auld."

"Ay, ye're gey auld," said Macgregor agreeably.

"But I'm no' that auld," said Mr Purdie hastily.

They took a seat facing the bay. Macgregor proceeded to haul in a tin steamboat which he had been dragging after him since they started on their walk, while his grandfather drew from its case a well-seasoned meerschaum, removed the newspaper plug and "dottle," laid the latter on the top of a fresh fill, and, at the expense of seven or eight matches, lit up.

"I see a boat comin'," exclaimed Macgregor, ere they had been seated for five minutes.

"Whaur? . . . Oh ay. But that's no' the richt boat. Wait till ye see a boat wi' twa yella funnels."

"I like rid funnels better nor yella yins. Whit wey is Maw comin' in a boat wi' yella funnels?"

"Yer Maw disna like the watter, an' the boats wi' yella funnels dinna come sae faur as the boats wi' rid funnels. That's jist the wey o' 't, Macgreegor. Ha'e! Pit thae in yer gab."

"I like peppermint lozengers," observed Macgregor, drawing in his breath to get the full effect. "I like leemonade, furbye," he added presently.

"Are ye dry?"

"Ay."

"Aweel, ye'll maybe get a botle afore we gang to the pier. Whit ha'e ye been dae'in to yer steamboat? It's a' bashed, see!"

"A laddie trampit on it," said Macgregor, holding up his toy. "But the string gaed roon' his leg an' coupit him, an' he gaed awa' greetin' Whit wey is there no' a baun'? he inquired, looking round at the bandstand.

"It's no' the season yet."

"Whit wey is't no' the season? I like a baun' wi' a big drum. Wull there be a baun' the morn, Granpaw?"

"Na, na. No' till the simmer. If ma hoast's no' better I'll maybe bide in Rothesay till the simmer, and then ye'll come back an' stop wi' yer granny an' me, an' gether wulks, an' dook, an' hear the baun'."

"Is yer hoast bad the noo?"

"Ay; it's gey bad at nicht, Macgreegor."

"I yinst had an awfu' sair hoast," said Macgregor thoughtfully. "I got code-ile. If ye wis takin' code-ile ye micht be better afore the simmer, Granpaw."

Mr Purdie smiled. "Wud ye like ma hoast to be better afore the simmer, Macgreegor?"

"Ay. I—I wud like to bide in Rothesay tae. I dinna like wulks, but I like pickin' them oot awfu'. I dinna like dookin', but I like paidlin'."

"I'm thinkin' I'll try the code-ile, Macgreegor."

"It's rale nesty to tak'. . . . But it micht mak' yer hoast better afore the simmer. . . . Rothesay's a nice place; is't no'? . . . I'm gaun ower to luk at the watter." The boy slipped off the seat, and, dragging his steamboat behind him, went over to the railings of the esplanade.

"Ye're no' to sclim up," cried Mr Purdie, rising in alarm. "If ye wis fa'in' in there ye wud be droondit."

"There an awfu' lot o' watter the day," remarked the boy as his grandfather put an arm round him.

"Ay, ye see the tide's in."

"Oh, there a wee fish! D'ye no' see it, Granpaw? There anither!"

"Ye've better sicht nor me. Noo, noo, ye're no' to lean ower that wey. Ye canna soom, ye ken. An' whit wud yer Maw say if ye fell in?"

"She wud gi'e me ile—no' the code-ile, but the ither ile. It's faur waur. I'm gaun fur to sail ma boat noo."

"Ye canna sail it there."

"Ay, can I! See!" Macgregor lowered his toy by the string till it touched the water a yard beneath them. After several partial swampings it was induced to float on a comparatively even keel. "It's soomin'!" he exclaimed in triumph as he jerked it about.

And then the string slipped from his fingers. He turned to his grandfather in dire dismay.

"Puir laddie," said Mr Purdie, looking about for help in the shape of a rowing craft.

"Ma boat, ma boat!" wailed Macgregor.

Old Mr Purdie went down on his knees, suppressing a groan as he did so, laid his pipe on the ground, and, leaning over the edge, endeavoured to secure the string with his walking-stick. For several minutes he wrought, but all in vain, and then Macgregor cried out that his boat was sinking. It was too true! Damaged, doubtless, by many a stormy passage on dry land, and also by being tramped upon, the luckless vessel had gradually filled, and now it was being slowly but surely submerged. Mr Purdie, in great distress, endeavoured to save it with his stick by getting a hold of the metal rigging, but his sight was poor and his hand shaky, and he only succeeded in giving it a prod amidships, which precipitated the disaster. Down, down, in ten feet of clear water it quietly sank, while its owner could do nought but watch and wail, "Ma boat, ma boat!"

Mr Purdie rose, rubbing his knees and coughing. "I'm rale vexed, Macgreegor," he began——

Crunch!

"Ma pipe, ma pipe!"

Alas! troubles never come singly. Macgregor had lost his beloved boat; Mr Purdie had trod upon and reduced to atoms his dear old pipe.

"Ma boat, ma boat!"

"Ma pipe, ma pipe!"

The boy gazed despairingly into the depths; his grandfather stared gloomily at the ground.

"Dinna greet, laddie," said Mr Purdie at last.

"I'm no' greetin'," returned Macgregor, rubbing his eyes with his sleeve and sniffing. Then he perceived the trouble which had befallen his companion.

"Whit wey——" he began, and stopped, stricken dumb by the distress in the old face.

"Macgreegor," said Mr Purdie, taking out a shabby purse, "ye'll maybe get yer boat when the tide gangs oot

I'll tell the man ower thonder to keep his e'e on it. An'—an' ye're no' to greet."

"I'm no' greetin', Granpaw."

"Aweel, I'm rale vexed fur ye. An' I wudna like ye to be meetin' yer Maw wi' sic a lang face. Ha'e! There a saxpence, Macgregor. Jist rin ower to the shopes an' buy onythin' ye ha'e a fancy fur, an' I'll wait fur ye here. Noo, ye dinna need to gang faur—jist ower the road. An' haste ye back, fur it's near time fur yer Maw's boat."

Having thus delivered himself, Mr Purdie heaved a big sigh and looked once more at the wreckage at his feet. The meerschaum had been a presentation, and he had valued it exceedingly. "It wis gettin' auld like hissel', but it wisna near dune yet," had been the substance of a frequent remark of his friends to him during the last five or six years. And now—now it was "dune."

"Are ye no' gaun to the shopes?" he asked his grandson, who was still looking at the sixpence.

"Ay. I'm gaun," said Macgregor. "Thenk ye, Granpaw," he added, remembering for once his mother's good instructions. And, his small visage wreathed in smiles of joyful anticipation, he ran off.

Mr Purdie saw him disappear into a fancy goods emporium, and then stooped down and gathered the fragments of his pipe into a large red handkerchief, which he carefully deposited in a side-pocket of his coat. After that he marked the place where Macgregor's toy had sunk, and toddled along to tell the nearest boat-hirer to look out for the wreck at low water. He was beginning to get anxious when Macgregor reappeared, jubilant, dragging behind him a clattering object.

"Did ye buy anither boat?" inquired Mr Purdie, feeling rather disappointed, for the boat-hirer had assured him that the wreck could easily be recovered.

"It's no' a boat," said Macgregor, smiling. "It's a beast."

"A beast?"

"Ay, Granpaw. A aggilator."

"A whit?"

"Aggilator! That's whit the wife in the shope said it wis. Luk at its taes! It can soom, but I'm no' gaun to pit it in the sea."

Mr Purdie examined the new purchase. "Oh, I see," he said at last. "It's whit they ca' a—a—a crocidile, Macgreegor."

"Naw, it's no' a crocidile, Granpaw; it's a aggilator."

"Weel, weel, it's a queer-like thing to buy, onywey; but if ye're pleased wi' it, that's a' aboot it. Noo, it's time we wis gaun to meet yer Maw."

Macgregor gave his disengaged hand to his grandfather, and they proceeded pierwards. Silently they went for a minute, at the end of which Macgregor remarked—"I didna spend a' my saxpence on ma aggilator, Granpaw."

"Did ye no'? Whit did ye pey fur't?"

"Fowerpence. I bocht a wheen strippit ba's."

"Did ye?"

"Ay, but I didna spend a' the tippence on them."

"Ye wud keep a penny fur yer pooch, like a wice laddie—eh?"

"Naw. I bocht ye a pipe, Granpaw," said Macgregor, grinning. He released his hand and dived into his pocket.

"Weel, I never!" said Mr Purdie, receiving a small paper parcel from his grandson. "To think the wean mindit me!" he murmured to himself. He patted Macgregor on the head and removed the paper.

"It's an awfu' nice kin' o' pipe, Granpaw," said Macgregor. "Ye pit watter intil't, an' then ye blaw, an' it whustles like a birdie!"

Mr Purdie fairly gaped at the instrument of torture in his hand. For a moment he seemed to be stunned. Then he exclaimed, "It bates a'!" and went into a fit of chuckling, which was only stopped by the advent of a "hoast."

"Dae ye like it, Granpaw?" asked Macgregor.

"Fine, laddie, fine!" said Mr Purdie when he had recovered his breath. "Dod, yer Paw'll ha'e a guid lauch when he sees ma new pipe. Ye'll ha'e to learn me to play on't, though."

"Ay, I'll learn ye," said Macgregor graciously, and looked much gratified at the prospect.

"Can ye see the boat comin'?" inquired the old man a little later.

"Ay. It's comin' frae the lichthoose."

"Weel, it'll no' be in fur a wee yet. We'll jist tak' a sate on the pier."

"Ay, Granpaw. . . . I'm gey dry."

"Tits! I near furgot yer leemonade. But we'll shin pit that richt, Macgreegor."

VI

"A CAYBINET GROWP"

It was evident that the Robinson family, as it tramped along Argyle Street that Saturday afternoon, was bent on business of importance. Lizzie and wee Jeannie were dressed in their best, which would take rather long to describe; Macgregor had on his Sunday suit and a new glengarry bonnet; and John wore his pot hat a little to one side, and suffered from a high, tight collar, the points of which nipped his neck every time he moved his head.

"Are we near there, Paw?" inquired Macgregor, looking up to his father's face.

John looked down at his son, smothered an exclamation of agony, and replied in the affirmative.

"Whit wey dae folk get likenesses tooken?" asked the boy.

"Dod, ye may weel speir, Macgreegor! It's yer Maw wants a pictur' to gi'e to yer Granpaw Purdie."

"I'm no' wantin' to be tooken, Paw."

"Are ye no', ma man? Deed, I'm gey sweirt masel'. But yer Maw wants the pictur'."

"Whit's that ye're sayin' to Macgreegor, John?" said Lizzie.

"Aw," replied her husband, turning to her, and wincing

as the collar bit him, "Macgreegor an' me wis thinkin' we wis feart fur the photygrapher."

"Oh, ay," said Lizzie with a good-humoured smile. "Aweel, wee Jeannie an' me'll no' let him hurt ye—wull we, ma doo? But whit's wrang wi' ye, John? Ye're makin' maist frichtsome faces!"

"It's the collar, wumman. Ye wud ha'e me to pit in on."

"It luks rale nice. Is't a wee thing ticht?"

"Dod, it's like to nip the neck aff me!"

"Never heed, John. It'll come oot fine in the photygraph. Mercy me! whaur's Macgreegor?"

They retraced their steps anxiously, and discovered their son standing on the kerb, gazing longingly at the barrow of a vendor of hokey-pokey or some such elusive dainty.

"Macgreegor, tak' yer Paw's haun', an' dinna let me catch ye stravaygin' awa' again, or ye'll get nae carvies to yer tea," said Lizzie, glad enough to have found the youngster so speedily.

"John," she added, "fur ony favour, keep a grup o' the wean."

"Come on, Macgreegor," said John, holding out his hand. "We're jist comin' to the photygrapher's."

Presently they began to climb a long, narrow stair.

"Gi'e wee Jeannie to me, Lizzie," said John.

"Ay; ye'll manage her better nor me. I'm no' wanting to be photygraphed wi' a rid face an' pechin'," said Lizzie, handing over her burden, on receipt of which John suffered fresh torments from his collar.

"Maw, wull I get ma likeness tooken wi' ma greengarry bunnet on?" asked Macgregor, as they toiled upwards.

"Ye'll see whit the man says," returned his mother.

"I'm no' wantin' him to tak' it aff."

"Weel, weel, ye'll see whit he says."

"Wull ye tak' aff yer ain bunnet, Maw?"

"That's a daft-like thing to be askin'."

"Whit wey——"

"Whisht! whisht!" said Lizzie, who was evidently anxious to save her breath.

At last they reached the top flat, and were accommodated with seats in the reception-room. Lizzie took wee Jeannie on her knee and proceeded to make the child as neat as a new pin, conversing with her the while.

"Paw," inquired Macgregor, staring at a number of photographs on the wall, "whit wey dae folk mak' faces when they get their likenesses tooken?"

"Thae's jist real faces," said John, laughing and putting his hand to his throat.

"Can I get makin' a face when I'm gettin' ma likeness tooken?"

"Yer Maw wudna like that."

"Whit wey, Paw?"

"Och, jist—jist because she wudna. See, Macgreegor, yer Maw's wantin' ye."

Lizzie beckoned the boy to her. "Macgreegor, pu' up yer stockin', an' dinna screw yer face like that. . . . Oh, laddie, whit wey did ye gang an' mak' yer heid sae toosie? Staun' till I get yer hair to lie." She fished a comb from her pocket and used it till she had reduced the unruly locks to order. "Noo, sit doon on that chair, an' dinna stir a fit till the man's ready fur us. John!"

"Weel, Lizzie?"

"Come ower here till I pu' doon yer jayket. It gars ye look humphy-backit."

"Hoots, wumman, I'm no' gaun to get ma back tooken," said John, coming over nevertheless.

"Ye never ken hoo ye'll get tooken," said Lizzie sagely. "I wis lukin' at some o' the picturs here, an' some o' them's no' jist whit I wud ca' inchantin'."

"Ye better no' let wee Jeannie see them, or she'll be gettin' frichtit. Eh, wee Jeannie, whit dae ye say, ma duckie?" he said, laughing and chucking his daughter under the chin.

"Paw!" exclaimed wee Jeannie. "Paw-aw-aw!"

"Fine, lassie, fine!" cried her father. He was in great

form now, his collar stud having given way a minute previously.

"Noo, yer jayket's lyin' better, John," said his wife. "But yer tie—oh, man, yer tie's awa' up the back o' yer heid!"

"I canna help it, wumman. If I pit on yin o' thae masher collars, ma tie slips ower it, as shair's daith!"

"But whit wey dae ye no' use the tabs?"

"Och, I'm fur nane o' yer tabs! Never heed, Lizzie, I'll pu' it doon masel'."

"Tits!" exclaimed Lizzie, "I near had it that time! Noo —noo I've got it. There!"

At the word of triumph the tie slipped into its place, but the collar flew open.

"Whit's ado wi' ye, John?" she cried a little crossly. "Whit wey did ye unbutton it?"

"The stud's broke!"

"The stud's broke? Oh, John, an' you gaun to ha'e yer photygraph tooken!"

"Ach, it's a' richt, dearie. I'll jist button my jayket, an' that'll haud it thegither. See, that's fine!"

"Oh, John," she began, but just then a voice requested the family to step into the adjoining room.

"Mind, John, it's to be a caybinet growp," whispered Lizzie as she took a last survey of wee Jeannie and Macgregor.

John explained his wishes to the photographer, and presently the group was arranged — Lizzie with wee Jeannie on her knee, Macgregor standing beside her with his toes turned well out, and John behind, with one hand resting affectionately on her shoulder. Then the photographer dived under the black cloth.

"Whit's he daein', Paw?" inquired Macgregor in a hoarse whisper.

"Whisht!" murmured Lizzie.

"He's spyin'," said John softly.

"Whit wey is he spyin', Paw?"

"Jist to see hoo we're a' behavin'," returned his father jocularly. "Eh, Lizzie?"

D

"Be quate, John!" whispered Lizzie severely. She was sitting very stiff and dignified. Wee Jeannie began to show signs of restlessness, but ere long the photographer re-appeared. He suggested that the little boy should remove his hat, and that the gentleman should open his jacket.

"I'm dune fur noo," muttered John, with a wry smile.

"Macgreegor, tak' aff yer bunnet," said Lizzie miserably, fearful of what would shortly happen behind her.

"I'm no' wantin' to tak' aff ma bunnet, Maw," said Macgregor.

"Dae whit ye're tell't. Ye can haud it in yer haun'."

"Yes, just so. Hold your bonnet in your hand, my little man," said the photographer pleasantly.

Macgregor obeyed sulkily.

"Kindly undo all the buttons—all the buttons, please," said the photographer to John with great politeness, and turned to the camera.

With a feeble snigger John undid the last but one. Lizzie's head had been sinking lower and lower. She felt she was about to be affronted.

"Maw," said Macgregor suddenly, "I—I've toosied ma heid. Wull I pit on my greengarry bunnet again?"

Lizzie looked up quickly, and whipped something from near her waist. "John," she said, "gang to the ither room, an' see if I left ma caim on the table." Her voice sank to a whisper. "An'—an' here twa preens." She turned to the photographer. "Ye'll excuse me keepin' ye waitin' a meenit, sir?" she said to him. "This laddie's a rale wee tease," she added softly.

The photographer smiled good-humouredly, and immediately she discovered that the comb was in her pocket after all. She tidied her son's hair carefully, and said, "I think I wud like him tooken in his bunnet, if ye've nae objections."

"Oh, very well," replied the man agreeably. "His expression was certainly happier with it than without."

John entered grinning, his jacket thrown open. "I cudna fin' yer caim ony place, Lizzie."

"Och, I had it in ma poket efter a'. Noo, we're ready, if ye please, sir," she said to the photographer, who, without delay, set about his business.

He waited till the smiles had died down somewhat, when he instructed them where and how to look, and made an exposure, which Macgregor spoilt by scratching his nose at the critical moment.

"I cudna help it, Paw. Ma nose wis that kitly," said the boy.

"Weel, ye maun jist thole the next time, Macgreegor. Noo he's gaun to tak' anither yin."

"Whit's that wee thing he scoots wi'?"

"Whisht!"

"Steady, please," requested the photographer.

Wee Jeannie began to wriggle on her mother's knee.

"Oh, see! oh, see!" said Lizzie, pointing to the camera. "Oh, see a bonny wee winda!"

"Paw, whit's inside the boax?" asked Macgregor.

"If you please," said the photographer. "Now when I say three.—One—two—th——"

"Am I tooken, Paw?"

"No' yet, Macgreegor, no' yet. Ye near spilet anither photygraph. Keep quate, noo."

"Noona, noona," said Lizzie, dandling wee Jeannie, who was exhibiting fractious symptoms. "Wee Jeannie's gaun to ha'e her likeness tooken i' the bonny wee winda! (My! John, I wisht I had brocht her auld jumpin-jake.) Oh, see! oh, see!"

A lull at last occurred, and the photographer took advantage of it; and, after another period of unrest, he secured a third negative, which he assured Lizzie would prove highly successful. John had expected to have the photographs away with him, but his wife informed him in a whisper that he mustn't think of such a thing. "Caybinet growps" took time. Matters having been settled, the family departed from the studio.

"Maw, wull my greengarry bunnet ha'e a rid toorie in the likeness?" inquired Macgregor.

"It'll no' be rid, onywey, dearie."

"Whit wey, Maw?" He was obviously deeply disappointed.

"Speir at yer Paw, ma mannie."

Macgregor repeated the question.

"Aweel, if it disna come oot rid," said John, "I'll ha'e it pentit rid fur ye. Dod, I wull, fur ye're jist a jool! Is he no', Lizzie?"

"Oh, wee toosie heid!" cried his mother, with a laugh and a sigh.

VII

GREEN PAINT

So far Macgregor had spent a delightful evening, although at first he had felt the absence of his devoted chum, Willie Thomson, who, unfortunately, was confined to his home with a swollen face, the result, probably, of a soaking received the previous day while hanging on behind a Corporation watering-cart, which he and Macgregor had too hastily assumed to be empty. But Macgregor had speedily found a companion in Hughie Wilson, a boy whom he had hitherto rather despised, but who on this occasion had proved himself quite worthy of notice, having in his possession a pea-shooter and a fair quantity of appropriate ammunition. Hughie made no objection to sharing his sport with Macgregor, and by the time nearly all the peas were fired away—with more or less painful and irritating effect on pedestrians and owners of windows—or chewed and swallowed by the sharpshooters, the twain were on the best of terms, and all might have been well, had Macgregor only refrained from bragging of and exhibiting his athletic prowess. The competitions, which were begun in a spirit of friendly rivalry, ended in a very different spirit so far as Hughie was concerned, for he had to suffer defeat in everything he attempted, and, while hiding his chagrin successfully enough, he was inwardly boiling with mortification and longing to discomfit his victor.

Macgregor, on the other hand, made no effort to conceal his elation.

"I tell't ye I wud bate ye," he said gleefully, as they walked away in the dusk at the end of the series of running and leaping trials.

"I'm no' heedin'," retorted Hughie, slipping a stray pea into his mouth. "Are ye gaun hame noo?"

"Ay," replied Macgregor, who had promised to be home by seven (it was now half-past that hour) to study his lessons. "But ye're no' vera quick on yer feet, Hughie," he continued pleasantly. "I'll ha'e to gi'e ye a guid stairt the next time we try a race. Eh?"

"Och, I'm no' heedin' aboot racin', nor jumpin' either," said the other carelessly. "I jist done it to please ye."

"Fine ham! Ye're jist sayin' that because ye got bate. D'ye mind thon time when I jamp near twicet as faur as yersel'? Eh? D'ye mind it?" Macgregor persisted.

"Naw!" said Hughie shortly.

"Ah, ye mind it fine!"

They walked several yards in silence, and Hughie said:

"Ye think ye're awfu' clever, but I'll bet ye onything ye like ye canna sclim a lamp-post."

"Whit's that ye're sayin'?"

"I'm sayin' ye canna sclim a lamp-post."

"Can I no'?" Macgregor cried. "I'll shin let ye see!"

"Weel, sclim thon yin," said Hughie, pointing to the lamp-post which they were approaching. "Speel up thon— if ye can!"

"I'll speel up it afore ye can whustle!" exclaimed the valiant one.

Hughie smiled, it might have been doubtingly.

"D'ye think I canna dae it?" roared Macgregor, thoroughly roused, flinging off his cap and jacket, and tossing them into a convenient entry.

Still smiling, Hughie edged away.

Macgregor spat lightly on his hands. "I'll shin let ye see!" he cried, advancing to the post.

At the moment he gripped it with hands and knees Hughie burst into a jeering laugh and, turning, bolted up the entry. But, as luck would have it, he tripped over his companion's jacket and fell; and the next instant Macgregor was on the top of him, kneeling on his back.

"Ye kent the pent wisna dry," Macgregor cried, half choked with rage. "I'll gi'e ye the best bashin' ye ever——"

"Aw—aw! Let me alane," howled the other, struggling desperately, and vainly endeavouring to protect his face and hair from the sticky green hands.

"Ye kent it wis wat pent," retorted Macgregor, with a vicious rub at an exposed patch of cheek.

"I didna! The—the man maun ha'e ta'en the ticket aff ower shin. It wis there the day."

"Wis't? Aweel, ye *thocht* it wud be wat yet."

"Aw, ma nose!" yelled the victim, as that organ received a smear. "I'll tell ma big brither on ye, and he'll——"

"Ye're to get a bashin' first. Ye'll get it as shin as I clean my haun's on ye. *There!* . . . an' *there!* . . . an'——"

A door close at hand opened, and a very respectable elderly woman appeared on the scene.

"Mercy me!" she exclaimed, horrified, "are ye fechtin', ye bad boys? Stop it this instant!"

Hughie redoubled his cries, but Macgregor continued his operations, totally regardless of the intruder.

"Oh, me!" groaned the old lady. "I wish ma man wis in the hoose. . . . Stop fechtin', like guid boys, if ye please," she implored, laying her hand on Macgregor's shoulder.

"Awa' an' bile yer heid!" was his rude command.

"He's killin' me," wailed Hughie.

Driven to desperation, she stooped and captured one of Macgregor's hands, whereupon the victim wriggled himself free, and rose to his feet, exhibiting so fearsome a visage that the would-be peacemaker cried out in horror and let go the victor. Before she realized the condition of her own fingers, and the wrist of one of her sleeves, she was alone, and Macgregor was in hot pursuit of Hughie. The latter, however, in this instance, won the race, reaching home a woeful and grotesque object.

Having given up the chase at the last moment, Macgregor returned, almost satisfied with his revenge, to the entry for his cap and jacket. It was not till he had recovered his property, which he did before his breath, that his attention was attracted to the condition of his knickerbockers. Even in the feeble lamplight the damage looked very, very serious, though it was confined to the cloth on the inner sides of his knees. The knickerbockers, too, were comparatively new, and he had put them on that afternoon to allow of his mother making some repairs upon his everyday ones. He remembered that she had warned him to be careful as to what games he played, and the flush of his recent excitement gave way before a chill of remorse and foreboding.

Although his home was just round the corner, it was nearly half-an-hour later ere he knocked at the door and was admitted by his mother.

"Ye've been ower lang ootbye, laddie," she said a little reproachfully, but not crossly. "Ye sudna furget the time when ye've yer lessons to learn. Is that pent I smell on ye?"

"It—it wis on ma haun's, but it's near a' aff," he returned, keeping his knees well together and exhibiting his palms. Fortunately it was not very light in the little lobby.

"Weel, I'm gled ye didna file yer claes, Macgreegor. Awa' an' wash yer haun's, an' then get stairtit to yer lessons. Ye'll never be dux if ye gang on like this."

Had her son been in his usual spirits, he would probably have retorted that he did not want to be dux, but on this occasion he followed her into the kitchen in silence.

"Here he comes wi' as mony feet's a hen!" cried his father jovially, looking up from his paper.

Macgregor smiled feebly in response, and with a gait not unlike that of the fowl just mentioned went over to the sink, where he washed long and diligently.

Immediately he had dried his hands he procured his lesson-book and took a chair as far from the fireside as possible.

"Dinna turn in yer taes like that, laddie," said his mother, who, to his relief, was preparing to go out on a domestic errand. "Onybody wud think ye wis deformed.

"Och, dinna fash yersel', Lizzie," put in her husband. "The wean's fine. He'll jist be easin' his legs efter rinnin' aboot. Wha wis ye playin' wi' the nicht, Macgreegor?"

"Hughie Wulson."

"Whit. wis ye playin' at?"

"Haud yer tongue, John," interposed Lizzie, "an' let Macgreegor pey attention to his lessons."

"Dod, ay," said John agreeably. "We mauna interfere wi' his lessons. Are ye gaun yer messages noo, Lizzie?"

"Ay. I'll no' be lang. I'm vexed I didna get them done afore ye cam' hame, but I wis gey thrang the day, an' Mrs M'Ostrich cam' in an' blethered half the efternune. She's gaun to ha'e anither pairty, but she's no' askin' Mistress Purdie."

"She's askin' Macgreegor, though."

"Macgreegor'll get, if he's a guid laddie. . . . Weel, I'll awa afore the shopes shut. Luk efter wee Jeannie, if she waukens, an' hear Macgreegor his spellin's, if he's ready afore I come back. . . . Macgreegor, whit wey ha'e ye gotten yer guid breeks a' twistit-like? Pu' them roon' at the knees, an' see an' learn the meanin's furbye the spellin's."

She hurried away, and silence reigned for a little in the kitchen.

John resumed his paper, but ere long he glanced over it at his son. He felt that all was not well with the youngster.

"Are ye wearit, ma mannie?" he asked kindly.

"Naw."

"Are ye no' weel?"

"I'm fine," replied Macgregor in a voice that belied his words.

Three minutes passed, and John took another glance.

His son was holding the lesson-book to one side, and

appeared to be examining with much minuteness the knees of his knickerbockers.

"Are ye no' comin' to sit aside me the nicht, Macgreegor?" John inquired, dropping his paper and stretching out a big inviting hand.

Macgregor hastily resumed his studies.

"Come awa'," his father went on. "I dinna like ye sittin' there as if you an' me had cast oot. . . . Are ye no' comin'?"

The youngster shook his head; then gulped slightly.

John got up and went over to where the penitent sat. "Macgregor, ye best tell us a' aboot it," he said gently. "Whit's vexin' ye, ma wee man?"

After a little while Macgregor explained his unhappy plight, easing at the same time his stiffened limbs.

"Puir laddie," said his father sympathetically. "It wis a dirty trick to play on ye," he added indignantly.

"I wiped ma haun's on his heid," Macgregor observed with some satisfaction, "an' I wud ha'e gi'ed him a bashin', if a daft auld wife hadna come oot an'——"

"It's a peety it wasna yer auld breeks," said John reflectively. "I doot yer Maw'll be sair pit aboot. . . . I wonder if we canna get them cleaned afore she comes hame. If I had a wee drap terpentine noo, I wud try it."

"There terpentine in the wee press ablow the jaw-box," said Macgregor eagerly. "She wis cleanin' ma auld breeks wi' some the day."

"The vera thing the doctor ordered!" his father exclaimed jubilantly, and went to the cupboard indicated.

"It's a black botle, Paw."

Just then wee Jeannie awoke and demanded attention. By the time her father realized that she was determined not to go to sleep again, the clock warned him that his wife might return at any moment.

He wrapped the child in a blanket and sat down with her on his knee by the kitchen fire.

"Here, Macgregor; bring ower the botle, an' we'll try what we can dae."

"Here the botle, Paw, an' here the wee bit flannen she rubs it in wi'."

"Tak' oot the cork then, an' let's smell to mak' shair it's terpentine—no' that I'm jist shair o' the smell. . . . Hph! Ay; I think that's richt. It's a wee thing like speerits o' wine, but that wudna dae hairm onywey. Weel, we'll ha'e to hurry up, or yer Maw'll catch us. Pit up yer leg, Macgreegor."

Macgregor did as commanded, twisting round the cloth so as to bring into position the splatch of green paint.

"Noo, ma mannie, haud the flannen till I pour a drap o' the terpentine on it—dinna jump like that, Jeannie daurlin' —an' then rub it on the pent. Are ye ready?"

"Ay, Paw."

"Aweel, here's guid luck to us a'!" And John with his one free hand cautiously tilted the bottle. "Steady, noo."

"Maw!" cried wee Jeannie with a bound of delight as a key rattled in the outer door.

Macgregor let cut a yell of dismay, while John groaned, "We're done fur noo! It's the wrang botle!"

Half-a-pint of lacquer, thickish and intensely black, was running leisurely down Macgregor's leg as Mrs Robinson, pleasantly smiling, entered the kitchen.

.   .   .   .

Lizzie's little whirlwind of wrath had passed, but her husband's wretchedness was not abated by the awful calm of her displeasure which had followed the outburst, and which now seemed as if it would last for ever.

Macgregor, after having his knickerbockers scraped with the back of a knife, had been sent ignominiously to bed, warned that he would be called to his lessons at half-past six in the morning, and informed that he had forfeited his last chance of getting to Mrs M'Ostrich's party or to any other entertainment which might occur during the approaching festive season.

"Ye canna gang ony place till ye get new breeks, an' that'll no' be this year, I warrant ye!" his mother had said.

"So ye needna be greetin' like a muckle tawpy, fur it'll no' gar me change ma mind."

"I'm no' greetin'," he had muttered, not without indignation, and had retired to his bed, where he lay miserably awake, swallowing the lump that always came back.

Wee Jeannie, also, had been smartly packed off to her nest, marvelling doubtless at her mother's unwonted sharpness towards her, but fortunately refraining from offering any vocal protest, and falling into placid slumber within five minutes.

By the fireside Mr Robinson sat silent, a spectacle of profound depression, glancing now and then at his wife, who, having laid her son's spoiled garment on a newspaper methodically spread upon the well-scrubbed deal table, was regarding the green and black stains with eyes from which all earthly hope seemed to have vanished.

"Lizzie," stammered John at last, breaking a wretched silence, "I'm unco vexed, wumman, to gi'e ye a' this bother. I—I done it a' fur the best."

"Aw, it's nae bother! I've naethin' else to dae, an' ye ken as weel as me that breeks cost naethin'," she returned with cold irony.

"But it wis jist a mishap, Lizzie."

"Deed, ay. I ken that fine. You and Macgreegor never dae onything wrang—it's aye jist a mishap! Jist that. Hooever, I sud be used to yer mishaps by this time. It's a' ma ain fau't fur gaun oot ma messages an' leavin' ye baith in the hoose. I sud ha'e got Mistress M'Faurlan frae next door to come in an' luk efter ye, the wey she used to dae when I had to leave wee Jeannie in the hoose alane. Oh, I'm no' blamin' you an' Macgreegor, fur it's no' to be expec'it ye can behave when naebody's takin' care o' ye. An' it's fine fun fur me! Ma enjeyment is mair nor I can describe!" Here she groaned.

"Ye're awfu' severe on a man, Lizzie," sighed her husband, after a short pause, wherein he suppressed a less humble remark.

"I wis speakin' aboot weans."

For a little while Mr Robinson held his peace.   Then he began to plead for his son.

"Ye see, Lizzie, it wis ma fau't.   Macgreegor never thocht of the terpentine.   *He* wisna fur tryin' to conceal his ain mishap wi' the green pent."

"Wis he no'?   Whit wey wis he turnin' in his taes an' twistin' roon' his breeks?"

"I wud ha'e done the same masel', Lizzie."

"I've nae doot ye wud."

"Tits, wumman!" he exclaimed, "whit wud *you* ha'e done?"

Mrs Robinson made no answer.   She took a shawl from a peg and threw it round her shoulders.

"Ye're no' gaun ootbye again at this time o' nicht?" said her husband in surprise.

"I'm jist gaun to the druggist.   He's open till ten."

"Are ye no' weel, wife?"

"I'm gaun to see if he's got onything that'll tak' oot yer mess.   Maybe benzine'll dae, but I doot it."

"I'll gang fur ye," John said eagerly.   "It maybe wudna be safe to leave me in the hoose, Lizzie," he added with an attempt at a laugh.

"Maybe ye're richt," she retorted coldly.   "Ye can gang, if ye like. . . . Tak' the breeks wi' ye.   Gang quick, fur it's near ten."

John put on his cap and made for the door.   There he halted for a moment.   "Try an' let Macgreegor aff this time," he whispered.

Lizzie heard the outer door shut quietly, and seated herself to wait her man's return.   It had been an extra hard day, and she nodded drowsily.

Presently she became aware that her son, barefooted and mournful of countenance, was standing beside her.

"Whit are ye wantin', Macgreegor?"

"I—I'm vexed, Maw."

"Muckle need! . . . Can ye no' sleep?"

"Naw. . . . It wis me to—to blame, Maw.   I—I tell't

him the wrang botle, an'—an' I didna ken the lamp-post
wis new pentit."

"But ye maun try to ha'e some sense, laddie," she said,
with diminishing severity.

"Ay, Maw; I'll try. . . . But dinna be vexed wi' Paw.
. . . I'm—I'm no' awfu' heedin' aboot Mistress M'Ostrich's
pairty, an' I'll learn ma lessons early in the mornin', an'—
an' I'll dae wi'oot taiblet on Setturday, an' tak' ile, if ye like.
But dinna——"

"Whisht, dearie!"

"But——"

Lizzie put her arm round him, and smiled reassuringly, if
a little sadly. "Ye're an awfu' laddie!" she murmured.
"Wull ye try an' be guid an' wice efter this? Eh?"

"Ay, Maw."

"Weel, gi'e's a kiss, an' awa' to yer beddy-baw. . . .
Come, an' I'll tuck ye in."

. . . .

Mr and Mrs Robinson sat later than usual that evening,
and did not seem to mind the atmosphere being redolent of
benzine, which, after all, was better than having it charged
with domestic electricity.

About eleven o'clock, when they were so comfortable
that it seemed a pity to retire, the door was cautiously opened
and Macgregor peeped in. He saw his parents before they
saw him, and his face lost its anxiety.

"Mercy me!" cried his mother, "ye're there again!"

His father smiled as one who has forgotten all his troubles.
"Whit wis ye wantin', ma mannie?"

Macgregor hesitated.

"Whit is't, dearie?" asked Lizzie kindly. "Ye sud ha'e
been sleepin' lang syne," she added.

The youngster took heart. "Is the pent aff ma breeks?"
he inquired.

"Vera near it," replied John. "Yer Maw's the clever yin!
She'll ha'e them as guid as new afore she's done wi' them."

There was a pause. Then—

"Wull I get to Mistress M'Ostrich's pairty?"

VIII

MRS M'OSTRICH GIVES A PARTY

"Och, wumman, I'm no' heedin' aboot Mrs M'Ostrich an' her pairty," said John, as he folded a strip of newspaper wherewith to light his pipe.

"Aw, but ye'll gang, John," said Lizzie persuasively.

"Are ye wantin' to gang yersel'?"

"Weel, ye see, it's no' as if I wis oot every ither nicht, an'——"

"Dod, then, we'll jist gang. I doot I whiles furget ye're in the hoose a' day; an' ye've had a gey sair time wi' wee Jeannie fur twa-three weeks. Ay, we'll jist gang."

Lizzie looked pleased. "When Mrs M'Ostrich wis in this mornin' to get the len' o' ma bew vazes, an' the mauve tidy wi' the yella paurrit on it, an' a wheen ither things, she says to me, says she: 'Mrs Robison, ye're weel aff wi' yer man'; and then she says——"

"Hoots!" interrupted John, "I'm thinkin' Mrs M'Ostrich is an auld blether."

"Auld blethers whiles say a true word," observed his wife. Then, fearing, perhaps, that she was expressing too much in the way of sentiment, she became suddenly practical. "I've a braw sark ready fur ye. I done it up the day."

"Am I to pit on ma guid claes?"

"Oh, ay, John."

"But no' a staun'-up collar?"

"Aw, John! An' I've a beauty jist waitin' fur ye. Ye luk that smairt in a staun'-up collar. I wis thinkin' o' that when I wis ernin' it, an' if ye had jist seen hoo carefu'——"

"Ach, Lizzie, ye get ower me every time! If ye wis tellin' me to gang to Mrs M'Ostrich's pairty wi' yin o' wee Jeannie's rid flannen goonies on, I wud jist ha'e to dae't!"

"Havers!" cried his wife, laughing the laugh of a woman who gains her point. "We'd best be gettin' ready shin."

"But whit aboot the weans?" asked John.

"Macgreegor's comin' wi you an' me. Mrs M'Ostrich said we wis to bring him, fur I tell't her I wis sweirt to leave him in the hoose."

"That's guid!" said her husband, with a smile of satisfaction. "Macgreegor likes pairties."

"I hope he'll no' affront us, John."

"Aw, the wean's fine, Lizzie. An' whit aboot Jeannie?"

"She'll sleep soun', an' Mrs M'Faurlan's comin' to sit in the hoose till we get back."

"I see ye've arranged it a'," he said good-humouredly. "Whit wud ye ha'e dune if I had said I wudna gang?"

"Ah, but I kent ye wud gang. . . . Ye micht rin doon the stair the noo an' get a haud of Macgreegor. He's ootbye playing' wi' Wullie Thomson. They've baith got sookers, an' they like fine when the streets is kin' o' wat. I dinna think sookers is vera nice things to play wi'."

"I yinst had yin masel', an' I near got the nick for pu'in' the stanes oot the streets. . . . Weel, I'll awa' an' see efter Macgreegor."

Later in the evening the trio set out for the abode of Mrs M'Ostrich, who, as Lizzie was wont to remark, "hadna muckle in her hoose, puir thing, but wis that fond o' comp'ny."

Mrs M'Ostrich, however, never had the least hesitation in borrowing from her friends any decorative article she did not possess, so that her little parlour on the occasion of one of her parties was decorated in really gorgeous style. Her chief trouble was her husband, who, being a baker, retired to the kitchen bed early in the evening, and snored with such vigour and enthusiasm that the company in the other room heard him distinctly. Mrs M'Ostrich had tried many devices, including that of a clothes-pin jammed on the snorer's proboscis, but all without avail. In the case of the clothes-pin, Mr M'Ostrich, who had meekly submitted to its being fixed, had suffered from a sort of nightmare, and, but half-awake, had startled a party in the parlour by frantic beatings on the wall and weird yellings to the effect that someone was trying to suffocate him. After that he was allowed to snore in peace, and Mrs M'Ostrich had to explain to any new visitors the meaning of the disturbance. This she did to John and Lizzie immediately on their arrival.

They were the last of the guests to appear, the six others being already seated round the parlour, doing a little talking and a good deal of staring at the decorations, the number and glory of which seemed to have quite paralysed a little woman who sat in the window.

"Maw," whispered Macgregor, who had been accommodated with a hassock at his mother's feet, "thon bew vazes is awfu' like oor yins."

"Whisht!" said Lizzie. . . . "As ye wis sayin', Mrs M'Ostrich———"

"Maw, there a tidy wi' a yella paurrit———"

"Whisht, Macgreegor!" said Lizzie, giving her son a severe look.

"He's a shairp laddie," observed Mrs M'Ostrich, who did not really mind, so long as her guests recognized only their own particular contributions to the grandeur of her surroundings.

"Awa' an' sit aside yer Paw, Macgreegor." said Lizzie. . . . "John, see if ye can keep Macgreegor quate."

The boy dumped his hassock over the feet of two of the company, and squatted beside his father. He felt rather out of his element among so many adults, most of them elderly, and he was disturbed to see his father looking so stiff and solemn.

A dreary half-hour went by, at the end of which he could keep silence no longer.

"Paw," he said to his parent, who was listening conscientiously to the long story of a Mrs Bowley concerning her husband's baldness, "Paw, whit's that noise?"

"Aw, never heed, ma mannie," replied John, aware that the noise proceeded from the slumbering Mr M'Ostrich. "It's jist a noise."

"It's awfu' like a big grumphy, Paw."

"Sh! Ye're no' to speak the noo."

"If I had a big grumphy——"

"Whit's the laddie sayin'?" inquired Mrs Bowley, smiling so kindly that Macgregor accepted her as a friend there and then.

"It's a grumphy," he explained confidentially. "Dae ye no' hear it?"

Mrs Bowley laughed, and patted his head. "Ye mauna speak aboot grumphies the noo, dearie," she whispered. "Here a bit sweetie fur ye."

Macgregor put the dainty in his mouth, and drew his hassock a trifle nearer to Mrs Bowley. "Ye're awfu' kind," he said in a hoarse undertone, and he and the good lady entertained each other for quite a long time, much to John's relief.

About half-past nine the company drew as near to the oval table as their numbers permitted, and did justice to the refreshments which the hostess had provided. Macgregor, ignoring his mother's warning glances, and evidently forgetting there was such a fluid in the world as Castor Oil, punished the pastry with the utmost severity, and consumed two whole bottles of lemonade.

"It's been an awfu' nice pairty, Paw," he whispered, when the chairs had been put back to the walls. "Are we gaun hame noo?"

Before John could reply, Mrs M'Ostrich requested the attention of the company to a song by Mr Pumpherston. All eyes were turned on a large, middle-aged man in a corner of the room, who wiped his brow repeatedly, and appeared very uneasy.

"Come awa', Mr Pumpherston," said Mrs M'Ostrich encouragingly. "Jist ony sang ye like. Ye needna be feart. We're nane o' us musical crickets."

"Ay, come awa', Mr Pumpherston," murmured several of the guests, clapping their hands.

"Is he a comic, Paw?" inquired Macgregor.

"Whisht!" said Lizzie, sighting danger ahead, and giving

E

John, beside whom she was now sitting, a nudge with her elbow.

Mr Pumpherston shuffled his chair an inch forward, fixed his eyes on the ceiling, and hummed, "Doh, me, soh, doh, soh, me, doh."

"Ay, he's a comic!" said Macgregor in a delighted whisper.

Someone sniggered, and John gently but firmly put his hand over his son's mouth.

"He's jist lukin' fur the key, as it were," observed Mrs Pumpherston, the little lady who had been overcome by Mrs M'Ostrich's parlour decorations. "He's whiles gey slow at catchin' the richt key, but he'll be gettin' it in a wee," she added, as her husband continued his "Doh, me, soh, doh, soh, me, doh," to the intense enjoyment of Macgregor, who quaked on the hassock in enforced silence.

At last Mr Pumpherston started *Ye Banks and Braes*, but when half through the first verse was compelled to stop and make search for a lower key.

"It's aye the wey wi' him," explained his wife. "But when yinst he gets the richt key he sings it weel eneugh, if he disna furget the words. . . . Ha'e ye got the richt key noo, Geordie?"

"I wis near it—but ye've pit me aff it. But I'll get it yet," quoth Mr Pumpherston determinedly. And he did get it eventually, and regaled the company in a voice surprisingly small for so large a man.

Macgregor was much disappointed, if not indignant, at being deceived, as he believed, by Mr Pumpherston; but presently, feeling drowsy, he climbed into his father's arms and dropped into a peaceful little doze. So he rested while several guests contributed songs, not all, by the way, such efforts as that of Mr Pumpherston.

Lizzie and John were congratulating themselves upon their son's good behaviour during the evening, and Mrs Bowley and another lady had just finished telling them what a "braw laddie" they were so fortunate as to possess, when Macgregor awoke, rubbed his eyes, and stared about him.

"Puir mannie, he's jist deid wi' sleep," remarked kindly Mrs Bowley.

"He is that," assented the other lady. "Are ye wearit, dearie?"

"There no' mony weans wud behave theirsel's like him," observed Mrs M'Ostrich.

Mrs Pumpherston said nothing, but smiled sourly. Probably the youngster's opinion that her husband was a "comic" still rankled.

"It's time ye wis hame, Macgreegor," said Lizzie, rising.

But Macgregor heard none of the foregoing observations. With a dreamy look in his eyes, he was listening intently. "I hear it, I hear it," he muttered.

"He's no' hauf wauken yet," said Mrs M'Ostrich.

"Whit dae ye hear, daurlin'?" inquired Mrs Bowley.

Macgregor rubbed his eyes again. "I hear it! . . . It's in the hoose! . . . It's ben the hoose! . . . Paw, tak' me ben till I see the big grumphy!"

For a moment there was a dead silence. But laughter was inevitable. Poor Mrs M'Ostrich, her face crimson, had to join in, but, as Mrs Bowley remarked to a friend next day, she was evidently "sair pit oot."

As for Lizzie, after a hasty apology and good-bye, she hurried John from the house, and never opened her mouth till they were in their own kitchen. On the departure of Mrs M'Farlane, who had taken good care of wee Jeannie, Macgregor, three parts asleep, was put to bed with scant ceremony, after which Lizzie collapsed into a chair, and looked long at her husband.

"Weel?" she said at last.

"Weel, Lizzie?" he returned, trying to smile. "Ye've had yer nicht oot."

"Ay. An' it's the last!"

"Tuts, havers!"

"John, I've been affrontit afore, but never like the nicht. Macgreegor——"

"Aw, the wean didna mean ony hairm. He sud ha'e been tell't aboot Mrs M'Ostrich's man."

"Oh, ye've aye an excuse fur Macgreegor. I'm—I'm naebody!"

"Lizzie, wumman!" He got up and went beside her.

"Ah, I'm no' to be cajoled that wey, John."

John said nothing; but he tried several other ways, and did succeed in "cajoling" her at last. She heaved a great sigh and smiled back to him.

"But, dearie, whit are we to dae wi' the wean?" she asked.

"Guid kens," said John.

And suddenly they both fell a-laughing.

IX

MACGREGOR'S NEW HAT

"I DINNA think I'll gang oot the day, John," said Lizzie. "Wee Jeannie's that girny. I doot I'll hae to gi'e her ile, puir doo. Ye sudna ha'e gi'ed her thon bit kipper last nicht."

"Och, Lizzie, it wis jist a tate the size o' yer nail."

"Weel, ye ken fine she's ower wee fur kippers, John. An' ye ken I wudna gi'e her that kin' o' meat masel'. I'm shair ye micht ha'e mair sense not to gi'e her everythin' she cries fur. But it canna be helpit noo."

"I'm rale vexed, wumman," said John. "I think I'll bide in the hoose. I'm no' heedin' aboot gaun oot the day."

"Na, na, John. Ye've got to tak' Macgreegor to the baun', fur ye promised the wean."

"Tak' Macgreegor yersel', Lizzie, an' I'll mind wee Jeannie."

"Toots, havers! Ye see, I'm no' jist shair if it wis the kipper that done it, sae ye needna be blamin' yersel' aboot wee Jeannie."

"Dae ye think it wisna the kipper?" said John eagerly.

"Maybe it wisna. Onywey, I ken whit to dae; sae aff

ye gang wi' Macgreegor. . . . Macgreegor, ha'e ye washed yer face?"

"Ay, Maw."

"Weel, bring ower the brush, till I pit yer hair stracht. . . . Staun' quate noo! Tits, laddie! hoo can I mak' a shed when ye're wagglin' yer heid? . . . There, noo! . . . Let me see yer haun's. Did ye wash them?"

"Ay, Maw."

"Awa' an' wash them again. An' tie yer lace. . . . Here, John, keep yer e'e on wee Jeannie till I get Macgreegor's new hat." Lizzie dived under the bed, opened a box, and brought out a parcel.

"Whit kin' o' bunnet's that?" inquired her husband.

"Wait an' ye'll see," returned Lizzie, smiling as she undid the paper. "The man said it wis an Alpine hat, an' vera genteel. Macgreegor's needin' a new hat. His glengarry's gettin' kin' o' shabby fur the Sawbath, sae he'll wear it every day an' ha'e this yin fur his guid yin. See! There the hat, John. It'll be a fine surprise fur Macgreegor. . . . Here, Macgreegor, come an' see yer new hat."

"It's a queer kin' o' hat fur a wean," remarked John. "It's liker a man's. Dod, it's jist like auld Mackinky's— him that used to write til the newspapers efter he gaed daft. A Macalpine hat, did ye say? Macgreegor, let's see ye in yer Macalpine hat!"

But Macgreegor, who had been gazing dumbly at the headgear for fully half-a-minute, suddenly exclaimed, "I'll no' wear that thing."

"Noo ye've done it!" said Lizzie in a sharp undertone to her husband. "Ye've pit the wean aff it wi' yer stupid talk. . . . Macgreegor, ma mannie," she said to the boy, "yer Paw wis jist jokin'. See, pit on yer braw new hat, an' then ye'll gang to the baun'."

"I'll no' wear it," said her son, retreating a step. "I want ma greengarry bunnet."

"Ah, but this yin's faur nicer nor yer glengarry. . . . Is't no'?" she demanded of John, giving him a warning glance.

"Aw, it's a vera nice hat," he replied evasively. Then,

feeling that he was failing in his duty, he gently recommended his son to submit. "Come awa', Macgreegor, an' dae whit yer Maw bids ye."

"I'll no' wear it," said Macgregor stolidly.

"Ye'll no', wull ye no'?" exclaimed Lizzie. "If ye'll no', ye'll jist!" And taking the boy by the arm she gently but firmly placed the hat upon his head.

At this indignity tears sprang to his eyes; but he cuffed them away, and stood before his parents, an exceedingly sulky little figure.

"It's the brawest hat he ever had," said Lizzie, regarding her purchase with intense satisfaction. "Is't no', John?"

"Ay; it's a vera braw hat," replied John, with feeble enthusiasm. "Dae ye think it fits him, though?" he inquired.

"Fits him? Deed, ay! It's like as if his heid had been made fur't! . . . Is it no' rale comfortable, Macgreegor?"

"I dinna like it," replied the boy. "I like ma greengarry."

"Och, ye'll shin get to like it, dearie. Ye micht gang to see the King wi' a hat like that on yer heid. . . . Noo, awa' wi' yer Paw to the baun', an' be a guid laddie, an' ye'll get somethin' nice to yer tea."

"Come on, Macgregor," said John, holding out his hand. "You an' me'll ha'e a hurl on the caur, an' maybe ye'll fin' oot whit I've got in ma pooch."

Lizzie nodded pleasantly as they departed, and John looked back and smiled, while Macgregor, though subdued, was apparently becoming reconciled to his novel headgear. During the car journey the twain were perhaps quieter than usual, but by the time they reached the park, where the band was playing, John had ceased casting covert glances at his boy's head, and Macgregor, with a portion of "taiblet" in each cheek, was himself again.

Macgregor greatly enjoyed the loud and lively passages in the music, but he was inclined to be rather impatient while the conductor waved his baton slowly and the instruments played softly or were partly silent.

"Paw, whit wey is thon man no' blawin' his trumpet?" he inquired during a lull among the brasses.

"I cudna say, Macgreegor."

"If I had a trumpet I wud aye blaw it. I wud blaw it hard!"

John was about to assure his son that he fully believed him, when he heard someone behind say:

"Jist luk at that, Mrs Forgie! Is that no' an awfu' daft-like hat to pit on a laddie?"

"It is that, Mrs Bawr. I wudna let a laddie o' mines gang oot in a thing like that fur a' the gold o' Crusoes."

John's ears tingled, and he nearly bit the end off his pipe. "Macgregor, I think we'll gang roon' and see the drummer," he said.

"Naw, I want to see thon man blaw his trumpet," said Macgregor, who, fortunately, had not heard his critics.

"Some folk," observed Mrs Bawr, "is gey fond o' tryin' to be gentry."

"Ye're richt there," assented Mrs Forgie, with a sniff. "I'm aye sorry fur weans that gets drest up like waux-works, jist fur to please their silly faythers an' mithers."

"Macgreegor," said John, "I'm no' gaun to wait fur the man to blaw his trumpet. I doot he jist cairries it fur show. Come awa' wi me." And, much to his surprise, the youngster was dragged away.

From that moment John's pleasure was at an end. Every smile he observed, every laugh he heard, seemed to have a personal application. Before the band performance was finished he and his son were on their way home, himself in mortal terror lest the boy should suffer insult. His worst fears were soon realized.

On the roof of the car Macgregor was chattering gaily when an intoxicated party inquired with a leer if he were aware that his hat was bashed. Macgregor shrank close to his father, whose wrath all but boiled over, and was very subdued for the rest of the journey.

As they walked along the street they were met by two small boys, who grinned at their approach, and laughed loudly behind their backs. John gripped the little fingers a thought closer, but held his peace.

Presently a juvenile voice behind them yelled, "Wha dee'd an' left ye the bunnet?" and another exclaimed, "Gentry pup!"

"Never heed, Macgreegor," whispered John.

"I—I'm no' heedin', Paw," said the boy tremulously.

Three little girls passed them, and broke into a combined fit of giggling. One cried "Granpaw!" after them, and the trio ran up a close.

But they were nearly home now, and surely the torment was at an end. But no! At the corner of the street appeared Willie Thomson and several other of Macgregor's playmates. They did not mean to be unkind, but at the sight of their little friend they stared for a moment, and then fled sniggering. And from a window above came a jeering hail: "Haw, you wi' the fancy hat!" followed by the impertinent exhortation—"Come oot the bunnet an' let's see yer feet." Finally, as they hurried into the familiar entry, a shout came after them, in which the word "gentry" was cruelly distinct. Climbing the stairs, John wiped the perspiration of shame and wrath from his forehead, while his son emitted strange, half-choked sounds.

"Never heed, Macgreegor; never heed," whispered John, patting the heaving shoulders. "Ye'll no' wear it again, if I've to buy ye a dizzen bunnets."

They entered the house.

"Ye're early back," said Lizzie cheerfully.

"Ay, we're early back," said her husband in a voice not familiar.

"Mercy me! Whit's a-do?" she cried. "Whit ails ye, Macgreegor?"

For a moment there was dead silence. Then Macgregor dashed his new hat on the floor. "I'll no' wear it! I'll no' wear it! I winna be gentry! I winna be gentry!" he moaned, and rushed from the house, sobbing as if his heart would break.

"De'il tak' the hat," said John, and, lifting his foot, he

kicked it across the kitchen, over the sink, and out at the open window.

Lizzie stared at her husband in consternation, and wee Jeannie, not knowing what else to do, started screaming at the top of her voice.

"Ha'e ye gaed daft, John?" gasped Lizzie at last.

"Gey near it," he replied. "See, Lizzie," he continued, "that hat's to be left in the street, an' ye're no' to say a word aboot it to Macgreegor. Listen!" And he proceeded to supply her with details.

"But it's a bewtiful hat, an' that genteel, an' I peyed—" she began ere he had finished.

"I'm no' carin' whit ye peyed fur't. I'd shinner loss a week's pey nor see Macgregor in anither Macalpine hat, or whitever ye ca' it. . . . Aw, Lizzie, if ye had jist seed the wey the puir laddie tried fur to keep frae greetin' when they wis makin' a mock o' him, ye wud——"

"Here, John, haud wee Jeannie," said Lizzie abruptly. "I maun see whit's come ower him. . . . Dinna greet, duckie. See if ye can keep her quate, John."

Lizzie was absent for a few minutes, and returned looking miserable. "I canna see him, John. Ye micht gang doon yersel'. He's maybe hidin' frae me," she said, with a sigh.

"Nae fear o' that, dearie. But he disna like folk to see him greetin'. That's why I didna rin efter him at first. But I'll awa' an' see if I can get him noo. An'—an', Lizzie, ye'll no' say onythin' aboot the hat? I'll bring it up, if ye want to keep it."

"Na. I'll no' say onythin', but it's a rale braw hat, an' that genteel, an' I doot somebody's rin aff wi' 't."

Just then Macgregor walked in, looking rather ashamed of himself, and with the tears scarcely dry. Yet, at the tenderly solicitous inquiries of his parents, he smiled as if he had been waiting permission to do so.

"Paw, there a——"

"Gi'e yer Maw a kiss," said John.

"Ye're an awfu' laddie," murmured Lizzie, cuddling him.

"Paw, there a wee——"

"Wud ye like a curran' cake to yer tea, Macgreegor?" inquired Lizzie, as she released him.

"Ay, Maw," he answered, beaming. Then—"Paw, there a wee dug ootbye, an' it's worryin' ma hat, an' it's pu'in' it a' to bits!"

X

A QUESTION OF PERSEVERANCE

"Can I get oarin', Paw?" said Macgregor from the stern, where he was sitting beside his mother and little sister.

"Dod, ay; ye'll get oarin'," replied his father, who was rowing leisurely and enjoying his pipe.

"Na; ye canna get oarin'," exclaimed Lizzie.

"Whit wey, Maw?"

"Jist because ye canna. Keep yer sate, noo, or ye'll ha'e the boat coupit."

"Aw, the wean's fine," said John. "If he wants to get oarin', let him——"

"Macgreegor maun bide whaur he is," returned Lizzie. "Near a' the accidents i' the papers comes o' folk changin' their sates. An' ye ken fine, John, I wudna ha'e come wi' ye the day if ye hadna' tell't me there wud be nae cairry-ons in the boat."

"Och, ye're awfu' easy frichtit," remarked her husband good-humouredly.

"Ay; I'm easy frichtit. Whit wud I dae wi' wee Jeannie if the boat wis capsizin'? I'm fur nae wattery graves, thenk ye, John!"

"Havers, wumman! Come on, Macgreegor, an' I'll learn ye to——"

"Dinna stir a fit, Macgreegor, or I'll——"

"I want to get oarin', Maw."

"Weel, I'm tellin' ye ye canna get oarin', an' that's jist a' aboot it! Luk at wee Jeannie noo, an' her that nice an' quate. She's no' wantin' to get oarin' an' ha'e us a' droondit —are ye, ma doo?"

Wee Jeannie continued to apply herself to a stick of barley sugar, and said nothing.

"She's ower wee fur to oar," said Macgregor scornfully. "Whit wey can I no' get oarin', Maw?"

"Michty me! Can ye no' tak' a tellin', laddie? See the yatts thonder! See thon big yin wi' the yella lum!"

"It's no' a lum; it's a funnel," returned Macgregor coldly.

"Aweel, it's a' yin," said his mother agreeably. "See thon steamboat comin' to the pier! Whit a reek! It's got yella lums—funnels—tae."

"I like rid funnels better nor yella yins. Can I get oarin' noo, Maw?"

"Tits, Macgreegor! I wunner at ye gaun on aboot oarin' when I've tell't ye ye canna. A fine job it wud be if ye coupit the boat, an' a whale got the haud o' ye!"

"There nae whales at Rothesay."

"Is there no?"

"Granpaw said there wis nane; an' he kens."

John chuckled. "He had ye there, Lizzie," he said. "Ye canna doot yer ain fayther's word."

"Aweel," said Lizzie, "there maybe nae whales as a rule, but nae man kens whit's in the sea, as Solyman says."

"Whales is feart fur folk," observed her son.

"The whale wisna feart fur puir Jonah, Macgreegor."

"If I had been Jonah——"

"Ye wud jist ha'e been ett up fur forty days and forty nichts."

"I wudna!"

"Ah, but ye wud! An' it wudna be vera nice in the whale's inside."

"I wud ha'e jaggit it wi' knifes an' preens till it let me oot," said the valiant Macgregor.

John laughed loudly, and Lizzie said reprovingly: "Ye sudna laugh when Macgreegor says sic daft-like things. Ye jist encourage him wi' his blethers an' boastin'. . . .

Macgreegor, I tell ye, if ye wis in the whale's inside ye wud jist be roarin' an' greetin' fur yer Maw."

"I wudna!"

"Ay, wud ye! Sae ye needna be boastin' aboot knifes an' preens."

"Wis Jonah roarin' an' greetin' fur his maw, Maw?"

"Ach, haud yer tongue! See thon wee boat wi' the sail."

"Whit wey has this boat no' got a sail, Maw?"

"It's got nae mast, ye see, Macgreegor," said his father.

"Whit wey has it no' got a mast, Paw?"

"Weel, ma mannie, it's jist a boat fur oarin'," said John.

"Can I get oarin' noo?" asked Macgregor.

"I'm shair I've tell't ye a dizzen times ye canna," cried his mother, who was engaged in fixing a fresh bit of paper to one end of wee Jeannie's barley sugar.

"When'll I get oarin'?"

"No' the noo, onywey."

"Wull I get oarin' in a wee while, Maw?"

"Ye'll no' get oarin' the day, sae ye needna be——"

"Wull I get oarin' the morn, Maw?"

"Oh, my! Wis there ever sic a wean? Deed, Macgreegor, ye wad spile the patients o' Job! Whit are ye wantin' to oar fur?"

"I jist want to oar."

"Let him oar, Lizzie," said John mildly.

"Na, I'll no' let him oar! An' I think ye micht ha'e mair sense nor to say 'let him oar' when I've tell't him fifty times he canna get oarin'."

"But the wean's that disappintit," urged her husband.

"Better disappintit nor droondit," quoth Lizzie shortly. "Whaur are ye gaun noo, John?" she suddenly inquired.

"Oot to get thon steamboat's waves," he returned, laying down his pipe and bending to the oars.

"Whit's that ye say?"

"I'm gaun to tak' ye oot to get a wee shoogy-shoo wi' thon steamboat's waves."

"I'm fur nane o' yer shoogy-shoos, John."

"Whit fur no'? Macgreegor likes a shoogy-shoo. Eh, Macgreegor?"

"Ay, Paw," replied Macgregor, roused from apparently gloomy reflections. "I like when the boat's whummlin' aboot."

"I'll whummle ye!" cried his mother. "Noo, John, ye're no' to dae't. We'll get sookit into the paiddles, as shair's daith!"

"Nae fears, wumman."

"Ah, but there is fears! I'm no' wantin' to get ma heid an' ma airms an' ma legs ca'ed aff, an' droondit furbye!"

"Wud the paiddles ca' wur heids aff?" inquired Macgregor with interest.

"They wud that," said Lizzie, relieved to see her husband altering his course.

"An' wud wur heids gang intil the ingynes?" pursued the youngster.

"Oh, haud yer tongue, Macgreegor!" cried his horrified mother. "Whit a notion fur a wean!" she observed to John.

"Paw, wud wur heids gang——"

"Whisht, laddie!" said his father. "Yer Maw disna like it."

"Whit wey?"

Getting no answer, he relapsed into a thoughtful silence, which lasted for about three minutes.

"Can I get oarin' noo?" he inquired.

"Here a boat wi' a rid funnel comin'," said John.

"Can I no' get——"

"Dod, there an awfu' crood on board her. D'ye see the folk, Macgreegor?"

"Ay. But can I no——"

"Ha'e, Macgreegor," said Lizzie, who had been fumbling in her pocket, "there a lozenger fur ye."

"Thenk ye, Maw," he returned, and remained quiet for a little.

Then—"Ma fit's sleepin'!" he exclaimed. "I want to dance."

"Ye canna dance here," said his mother. "Rub yer leg an' dunt yer fit on the floor. But dinna get aff yer sate."

Macgregor rubbed and dunted for some time, but without obtaining relief. "It's fu' o' preens an' needles, an' it's gettin' waur," he complained.

"Weel, ye maun jist thole it, fur ye canna get up an' dance in the boat," said Lizzie, not unsympathetically. "Try wagglin' yer leg, dearie."

Macgregor waggled violently, but to little purpose. His countenance expressed extreme discomfort. "It's awfu' jaggy," he said several times.

"Puir laddie," said his father. "It's a nesty thing a sleepin' fit. Is't no', Lizzie?"

"Ay, I mind I yinst had it in the kirk, an' I wis near dementit. Is't no' gettin' better, Macgreegor?"

"Naw; it's gettin' waur."

The parents became quite concerned about the sufferer.

"I doot ye'll ha'e to gang to the shore, John," said Lizzie, "an' let him get streetchin' hissel'!"

"Ay, he's got crampit wi' sittin' there sae lang. Weans isna used to sittin' quate. Is't rale bad, ma mannie?"

"A' ma leg's jaggy noo," replied the boy.

"Lizzie," said John suddenly, "if the wean wis gettin' oarin' fur a wee, dae ye no' think——"

"Na, na. I canna thole folk gallivantin' aboot in boats. Mercy me! there folk droondit every day jist wi' changin' their sates."

"I cud creep to the ither sate, Maw," said Macgregor, who had suddenly ceased rubbing, dunting, and waggling.

"An' he's ower wee, furbye," objected Lizzie.

"I'm no', Maw. Wullie Thomson's wee-er nor me, an' he aye gets oarin'."

"Is yer fit better?" asked Lizzie.

"Naw," said her son, hastily resuming operations. "Wullie Thomson's maw lets him oar," he added.

"I suppose ye wud shinner ha'e Wullie's maw nor yer ain," she said, glancing at her husband.

Apparently Macgregor did not hear.

"D'ye hear whit yer Maw's sayin', Macgreegor?" said John. "She's speirin' if ye wud like Mrs Thomson fur yer maw instead o' hersel'."

"Nae fears," said Macgregor promptly. "I like ma ain Maw best."

"Ye're an awfu' laddie," sighed Lizzie. "Wull ye be rale canny if I let ye get oarin'?"

XI

FOR WEE JOSEPH

OLD Mr Purdie placed his closed hands behind his back, and, with a twinkle in his eye, delivered himself of the ancient rhyme:

> "Neevy, neevy, nick nack,
> Which haun' will you tak'?
> Tak' the richt, or tak' the wrang,
> An' I'll beguile ye if I can!"

"I'll tak' the richt, Granpaw," said Macgregor.

Mr Purdie extended the member mentioned, disclosing a slab of toffee done up in transparent paper. "Ye're a rale smairt laddie!" he observed with a chuckle. "Ye aye guess whaur the gundy is."

"Ay, I'm gey fly," returned Macgregor modestly, beginning an onslaught on the sweetmeat.

Mr Purdie chuckled again, and slipped the packet of toffee which had been concealed in his left hand into his pocket.

"I'm aye richt, am I no'?" inquired his grandson.

"Ay, are ye, Macgreegor! It bates me to think hoo ye ken."

"Aw, I jist ken. . . . It's awfu' guid!"

"Is it?"

"Ay. I'll gi'e ye a taste."

"Na, na," said Mr Purdie, looking pleased. "I'll jist ha'e a bit smoke to masel'. Ye're no' to tell yer Maw I wis gi'ein' ye gundy, though; an' ye're no' to let it spile yer tea."

"I'll never let bug, Granpaw," said Macgregor, as if to set his relative's guilty conscience at rest.

The twain had come down to the shore at low water, and Mr Purdie was resting on a rock, while Macgregor hunted among the stones and seaweed for small crabs, several of which he had already secured and confined in an old battered meat tin.

"Noo, dinna get yer feet wat, laddie," said Mr Purdie, when he had got his pipe, a highly-seasoned clay, well alight.

"Nae fears, Granpaw," returned the boy reassuringly. As a matter of fact, his feet at the very moment were squelching in his boots. "Here anither!" he exclaimed, holding up a tiny crab. "It's awfu' kitly," he added, as he allowed it to run on the palm of his hand. "It's ower wee fur to nip. Wud ye like to fin' it in yer haun', Granpaw?"

"Deed, ay," said Mr Purdie, with the desire to please his grandson. "Ay, it's gey an' kitly. An' whit are ye gaun to dae wi' a' thae partins?" he inquired, indicating the meat tin.

"I'm gaun to tak' them hame."

"No' to Glesca?"

"Ay, to Glesca!"

"Aw, but they'll jist dee, Macgreegor."

"Whit wey?"

"Partins winna leeve in Glesca."

"Whit wey wull they no'?"

"They need saut watter."

"I'll tak' saut watter hame. I'll tak' it in a botle, Granpaw."

Mr Purdie shook his head, and the boy looked disappointed.

"Whit wud ye dae wi' partins in Glesca?" asked the former.

"Naethin'."

"An' whit wud ye tak' them hame fur?"

"It wisna fur masel'. I'm no' heedin' aboot partins. I wud be feart fur them growin' big an' creepin' intil ma bed. It wis wee Joseph wantit partins."

"Wha's wee Joseph?"

"He's a wee laddie. He's faur wee-er nor me, an' he's lyin' badly, an' his paw's deid, an' his maw washes."

"Ay, ay. An' sae wee Joseph wantit ye to bring him partins?"

"He wantit a monkey first; he thocht there wis monkeys at Rothesay, sclimmin' up the rocks an' rinnin' aboot the pier an' the shore. Wee Joseph never seen the sea."

"That's peetifu'. An' ye tell't him there wis nae monkeys?"

"Ay; an' he begood to greet. An' I tell't him aboot the partins, an' he said he wud like a wheen partins, an'—an' I thocht the partins wud leeve in Glesca, an'—an'—I'll jist tim them oot an' bash them wi' a stane."

"Na, na. Ye mauna dae that, Macgreegor," exclaimed Mr Purdie hastily. "The puir beasties canna help no' bein' able to leeve in Glesca."

"I'll bash them," cried Macgregor violently.

"Haud on, laddie, haud on. If you wis a wee partin, hoo wud ye like if a big laddie cam' an' bashed you wi' a stane?"

"If I wis a partin, I wud leeve in Glesca." And the youngster's eyes moved in search of a suitable stone.

"Macgreegor," implored the old man, laying his pipe on the rock, and rising, "dae ye think wee Joseph wud like ye to bash the partins?"

"Ay, wud he!"

"I'm shair he wudna. The puir wee partins never done onybody hairm."

Macgregor picked up a small boulder, remarking, "Partins nips folks' taes when they're dookin'."

"Ay; but no' wee partins like thur."

"Thae wee yins'll growe big," said Macgregor coldly.

F

"I'll bash this yin first," he added, selecting a poor little specimen from the tin, and laying it on the rock.

Grandfather Purdie seized the uplifted arm. "Macgreegor," he said gently, "ye're no' to dae it."

"Whit wey?"

"Because," said the old man, searching for an argument that might appeal to the young savage, "because it's sic a wee bit thing."

"It's gey wee," admitted Macgregor, peering into the tin while the victim slid off the rock and escaped; "ay, it's gey wee. Here a bigger yin. I'll bash it!"

"Macgreegor," said Mr Purdie solemnly, "ye mauna be crool. Ye wudna like if a muckle giant got a grup o' yersel', an' wis gaun to bash ye wi' his club."

"It's a' lees aboot giants. There nae giants!"

"Aweel, ye're no' to be crool onywey," said Mr Purdie, at a loss. "Let the wee partins rin awa', an' dinna vex yer Granpaw. The wee beasties is that happy, ye ken, an' it wud be a sin to bash them. They're jist like weans doon at the coast fur the Fair, rinnin' aboot an' enjeyin' theirsel's, an' they'll be awfu' obleeged to ye fur no' bashin' them."

The old man had evidently struck the right chord at last, for Macgregor dropped the stone, and said: "Weel, I'll no bash them, Granpaw."

"That's a fine laddie!"

"An' I'll let them awa'," he added, turning the tin upside down.

Mr Purdie patted the boy's cheek. "I kent ye wudna be crool," he said tenderly. "Here anither bit gundy fur yer gab."

"Thenk ye, Granpaw."

"An' ye'll never think o' bashin' partins again, Macgreegor?"

"Naw. But—but wee Joseph'll be unco sorry."

"Aha! But we'll ha'e to see aboot somethin' fur wee Joseph. Whit d'ye think he wud like?"

"He wantit somethin' that wis leevin'."

"Leevin'? Dod, that's no' sae easy," said Mr Purdie, resuming his seat and pipe, and gazing thoughtfully across the bay. "I ken a man here that keeps birds," he remarked at last. "Wud wee Joseph like a bird, think ye?"

"Naw," Macgregor firmly and unhesitatingly replied.

"A bird wud be a nice pet fur a laddie that's lyin' badly. It wud cheep an' sing til him, ye ken."

"Birds is ower easy kill't. Ye canna play wi' birds i' yer bed."

"Deed, that's true. . . . Whit think ye o' a wee cat? Mrs M'Conkie the grocer has got kittens the noo."

"Joseph had a wee cat, an' it scartit his nose, an' his maw pit it oot the house. He had white mice anither time, an' they had young yins, but his maw wudna let him keep them in the bed."

"Weel," said Mr Purdie, "I'm shair I dinna ken whit to say, Macgreegor."

"The partins wis best, if they wud ha'e leeved. Wee Joseph wis fur keepin' them in a boax, an' him an' me wis gaun to mak' them rin races on the blanket. Maybe they wud catch their feet in the ooss, though."

"I doot they wud, puir beasties. . . . But I'm fear't we canna get Joseph onythin' that's leevin'."

Macgregor looked depressed, whereat his grandfather sighed helplessly, and let his pipe go out.

"Ye see, laddie, there's no' mony things ye can gi'e til a wean that's lyin' badly," said the old man. "Wull Joseph be better shin?"

"Naw. It's his back that hurts him. He's awfu' bad whiles. I wudna like to be him."

"That's maist peetifu'! I'll tell ye whit we'll dae, Macgreegor."

"Whit, Granpaw?"

"We'll ha'e a keek at the shopes afore we gang hame to wur tea, an' ye'll maybe see somethin' that wud please him."

"Wull we gang noo?" exclaimed the youngster, brightening.

Mr Purdie consulted a fat silver watch. "Ay, we'll gang noo, an' see whit we can see. Gi'e's yer haun', Macgreegor. . . . Hech, sirs! but ye're no' to gar me rin. I'm no' as soople as yersel', ma mannie. Mind yer feet, or we'll baith be tum'lin' on the slippy places."

Without mishap, however, they came to the road, and soon reached the town, Mr Purdie "pechin'" and Macgregor beaming with anticipation.

At a window which seemed to be stocked with all the toys and trifles in creation they paused and gazed.

"Ha'e," said Mr Purdie, producing his purse, "there a thrup'ny-bit. Jist tak' yer pick, Macgreegor."

"Thenk ye, Granpaw. Oh, whit'll I buy?"

"Wud ye no' like to buy thon braw joog wi' the pictur' on it?"

"Naw."

"I'm thinkin' it wud be a nice kin' o' thing fur Joseph. Ye see it's got 'A Present frae Rothesay' on it; an' he wud like gettin' his tea oot o' 't. Eh?"

"Naw."

"Aweel, ye maun please yersel'. There a pent-boax noo. Wud Joseph like to pent, think ye?"

"Naw. I like pentin'—I'm gaun to be a penter when I'm a man. But I'm gaun to ha'e pots o' pent an' big dauds o' potty."

"Weel, maybe wee Joseph——"

"Naw."

"There a pretty pictur' book," said Mr Purdie. "Dae ye think——"

"Naw."

The old man gave up.

"I'll buy thon trumpet," cried the boy at last.

"I doot, when wee Joseph's lyin' badly, he'll no' be vera fit to blaw a trumpet."

"I cud blaw it fur him, Granpaw. I can blaw rale hard."

"Ay, but I'm feart wee Joseph michtna like that."

"Whit wey?"

Mr Purdie was about to attempt explaining, when suddenly Macgregor gave vent to a cry of delight. "See! —oh, see! there a monkey hingin' in the corner!"

"Haste ye an' buy it," said his grandfather, laughing.

Macgregor required no second bidding, and a couple of minutes later he was exhibiting his purchase. It was an earthenware monkey that bounded merrily at the end of a piece of elastic. "It's gey near leevin', is't no'?" he demanded. "See it loupin'!" And he continued to play with it until they were nearly home.

"Wee Joseph'll be unco gled to see it. It'll gar him lauch, puir laddie," said Mr Purdie.

"Ay," assented Macgregor, without much animation. For the moment he had somehow forgotten all about wee Joseph. He wound the elastic carefully about the monkey's neck, and walked on in silence.

"Ye'll like gi'ein' it to the puir laddie," said Mr Purdie, glancing down.

"Ay," answered Macgregor in a dismal whisper.

XII

AT GRANPAW PURDIE'S

THE Robinson family were spending the week-end at old Mr Purdie's Rothesay residence, but, much to their disappointment, the weather had completely broken down an hour after their arrival. Macgregor stood at the window, gazing disconsolately at the misty bay, while his elders— wee Jeannie having been put to bed—talked of matters which seemed to him totally void of interest.

"Can I get gaun ootbye noo?" he inquired at last of his mother, who was busily knitting and talking to Grandma Purdie.

Lizzie glanced at the window. "Deed, Macgreegor, ye needna be speirin' aboot gaun oot the nicht."

"It's no' sae wat noo, Maw."

"I'm thinkin' it cudna be muckle waur, dearie. Ye wud be fair drookit in hauf a meenit. Jist content yersel' in the hoose, an' ye'll maybe get a fine day the morn."

"I want to gang to the pier an' see the steamboats comin' in, Maw."

"Aweel, I'm rale vexed fur ye, but ye're no' gaun ower the door the nicht. Whaur's yer graun pictur'-book?"

"I seen a' the pictur's."

"Puir laddie," said Grandma Purdie, "it's no' vera cheery fur him sittin' in the hoose a' nicht. John, can ye no' divert the wean a wee? Gi'e him a bit ride on yer fit, man."

"Come on, Macgreegor!" his father cried willingly. "Come awa' and ha'e a ride on ma fit."

"Ach, he's ower big fur that kin' o' gemm," said Grandpa Purdie, noticing that Macgregor did not appear to appreciate the invitation. "Are ye no', ma mannie?"

"Ay," muttered Macgregor.

"Wud ye like to build hooses wi' the dominoes?" inquired the old gentleman.

Macgregor shook his head.

"Weel, wud ye like to build castels wi' the draughts?"

Macgregor shook his head again, and looked gloomier and more ill-used than ever.

"I ken whit Macgreegor wud like," put in John. "Him an' me kens a fine gemm. I'll be a draygon, an' hide in ma den ablow the table, and Macgreegor'll hunt me. I'll mak' him a spear oot o' ma *Evenin' Times*, an' he'll stab me till I'm deid. Eh, Macgreegor?"

"Fine!" exclaimed Mr Purdie.

"Preserve us a'!" cried Mrs Purdie.

"Oh, John and Macgreegor whiles ha'e fine gemms at the draygon," said Lizzie pleasantly. "But it's unco sair on John's breeks; an' he's got on his guid claes the nicht. . . . Pu' them up a wee, John, sae as no' to spile the knees."

"A' richt, wumman," replied John, as he rolled his newspaper into a harmless weapon. Presently he handed it to his son, and disappeared under the table, where he covered his head with a red woollen tidy.

"Come on, Macgreegor; I'm ready fur ye noo!" he shouted, and proceeded to emit fearsome noises.

"It bates a'!" Grandma Purdie cried, quite excitedly. "Whit a gemm!"

"John," said Lizzie, "did ye pu' up yer breeks?"

"Hoo can a draygon pu' up breeks?" returned her husband; and he resumed his growlings and groanings, while Macgregor began to stalk his prey with great caution and stealth.

"See an' no' pit oot yer Paw's een," said old Mrs Purdie, a trifle nervously.

"Gi'e the draygon a bit jab, an' gar him come oot his den," said Mr Purdie. "Dod, if I wis jist a wee thing soopler, Macgreegor, I wud mak' ye anither draygon."

Just then the dragon made a claw at the leg of the hunter, who let out a piercing yell and lunged wildly with his spear, without, however, getting it home. The fun became fast and furious.

"Come oot yer den, ye auld draygon, till I bore a hole in ye!" yelled the bold Macgregor.

"Gurr—gurr!" said the dragon, suddenly appearing on the other side of the table.

At this point the door opened, and Aunt Purdie stepped in. "What's ado, what's ado?" she inquired, rather sourly. John rose from the floor, trying to look at his ease, and Macgregor, the spirit of play chilled, shook hands dutifully with his relative and straightway retired to the window.

Aunt Purdie, whose husband's grocery business was still rapidly increasing, had taken rooms in Rothesay, not far from the old folks, for July and August. She was much too superior and proper a person for the Robinsons, and she was Macgregor's pet aversion. As Lizzie was wont to say, she was "rale genteel, but awfu' easy offendit."

"I was intending to go to the pier for to meet Robert," she observed as she sat down, "but it was that wet I jist came in to wait."

"Ye're rale welcome," said Grandma Purdie kindly. "Whit boat is Rubbert comin' wi'?"

"Robert is coming in the seven o'clock P.M. train from Glasgow. He cannot leave the shope any earlier the now."

"Weel, he'll no' be complainin' if trade's guid," said Mr Purdie brightly. "He'll ken to come here for ye the nicht, nae doot."

"Yes," said Aunt Purdie. Then turning to Lizzie, but speaking so that everyone in the room might hear, she said: "I've jist received a letter from my friend, Mrs M'Cluny."

"Ha'e ye?" returned Lizzie politely. She knew that she was about to be treated to news of her sister-in-law's grand acquaintances, in whom she had not the slightest interest.

"M'Cluny!" exclaimed old Mr Purdie. "Dod, but that's a queer-like name to gang to the kirk wi'! It's liker Gartnavel."

"It is very old Highland," said Aunt Purdie, with dignity.

"Ten year in botle," muttered John, with a snigger, whereat Mr Purdie slapped his knee and laughed loudly.

"Mrs M'Cluny," went on Aunt Purdie, "informs me that Dr M'Cluny has got to leave Glasgow."

"Wha's he been killin'?" asked Mr Purdie, and John stifled a guffaw.

"Haud yer tongue, man," whispered old Mrs Purdie, fearing lest her son's wife should take offence, as she had done too often before.

"Dr M'Cluny," the visitor continued, "has received an appintment in England. It is a very good appintment, but I'm sure I don't know what we are to do wanting Mrs M'Cluny when the winter season begins."

"Dis she gi'e awa' coals an' blankets?" inquired Mr Purdie, with a serious face.

The lady glanced at him sharply. "I was referring to Mrs M'Cluny's social—a—poseetion," she said stiffly. "We shall miss her greatly at our parties and conversonies. She was that genteel—I might even say autocratic. Her

and me is great friends, and we have been often com-
plimented for our arrangements at entertainments when we
was on the commytee. Everybody says Mrs M'Cluny is a
capital organism."

"Deed, ye'll jist ha'e to tak' her place when she's awa',"
said Mr Purdie, winking at John.

"Well, I must do my best," returned Aunt Purdie
modestly. "Of course, it has always been against Mrs
M'Cluny that her husband kep' a doctor's shope," she
added.

"Bless me, wumman, whit's wrang wi' that? If a man's
gaun to tell folk to tak' pooshun, he micht as weel sell it,"
cried the old man.

"It is not conseedered the proper thing by the best
people."

"Havers! Yer ain man keeps a shope."

"A grocery establishment," said Aunt Purdie, "is a
very different thing from a doctor's shope. I've never
heard tell of a man with a doctor's shope getting a title
from the hands of his Royal Majesty."

Mr Purdie burst out laughing. "Ca' canny, wumman,
ca' canny! I doot oor Rubbert's no' the lad to heed aboot
titles. Hoots, toots! . . . Come ower here, Macgreegor,
an' gi'e's yer crack," he said, anxious to get Aunt Purdie off
her high horse.

Macgregor came over from the window and leant
against the old man's knees. "Dae a recite, Grandpaw,"
he whispered.

"Eh? Recite?" The old man was pleased, however.
"Weel, I'll gi'e ye a bit readin', if ye like, Macgreegor,"
he said, putting on his specs and taking an ancient and
somewhat battered *Bell's Reciter* from a shelf at his elbow.
"Whit'll I read ye, ma mannie?"

"Read aboot the man that wis lockit in the kist till he
wis a—a—a skeletin, an' loupit oot on the ither man."

"The Uncle?"

"Ay. I like that yin awfu'!" said Macgregor, with a
shudder of anticipation.

"Whit's that?" cried Lizzie. "Aw, yer no' to read him that yin, fayther. He had an unco bad nichtmare the last time."

"It wisna the skeletin done it, Maw," appealed the boy. "It wis the pease-brose I had to ma supper. I aye dream when I get pease-brose—an' ile."

"He's sleepin' wi' me the nicht," put in John. "Ye'll no' be feart wi' me, wull ye, Macgreegor?"

"Naw!"

After some discussion, Lizzie reluctantly gave in, and Mr Purdie proceeded with the reading, which, as a matter of fact, had little interest for Macgregor until the final tragedy was reached. Then, while the old man, short of breath, gasped the lines and gesticulated in frightsome fashion, did Macgregor stand with rising hair, open mouth, and starting eyeballs, quaking with delicious terror. And hardly had the words "a sinner's soul was lost" left the reader's lips when the boy was exclaiming:

"Dae anither recite, Granpaw, dae anither recite!"

"Na, na, laddie. Nae mair."

"Aw, ay. Jist anither. Dae the yin aboot the man that stabbit the ither man wi' a jaggy knife, an' hut him wi' a stane, an' pit him in the watter, an' wis fun' oot, an' got the nick. Dae that yin."

After a brief rest Grandpa Purdie was prevailed upon to read "Eugene Aram's Dream," at the close of which he suggested that Macgregor should give a recitation.

"I'll gi'e ye a penny, Macgreegor," he said encouragingly.

"An' I'll gi'e ye anither," said John.

"An' I've a poke o' mixed ba's," added Grandma Purdie.

"Naw, I canna," said Macgregor.

"Come awa', ye can dae it fine," said his father. "Dae the recite yer Maw teached ye aboot the laddie on the burnin' boat."

"It wis an awfu' job gettin' him to learn it," remarked Lizzie.

"Weel, let's hear a' aboot it," said Mr Purdie.

"Och, it's a daft recite, an' I canna mind it," returned Macgregor.

"Ah, but we're a' wantin' to hear it," said Grandma Purdie. "Come awa', like a clever laddie."

"Ye can mind it fine," remarked Lizzie. "Ye needna be sae blate."

"I've a thrup'ny bit in ma purse," said Mr Purdie.

"Dod, I've yin, tae," said John.

The bribery was too much for Macgregor. "I'll dae't!" he exclaimed.

Everyone applauded, except Aunt Purdie, who muttered something about "bringing up children foolishly." Whereupon Lizzie murmured something about "talkin' o' bringin' up weans when ye ha'ena got ony!"—an observation which the other pretended she did not hear.

"I'll no' dae the yin aboot the burnin' boy," said Macgregor suddenly.

"Weel, dae anither," said his grandfather.

"He disna ken anither," his mother interposed. "It tuk me sax month to learn him the——"

"Ay, I ken anither. I learnt it frae Wullie Thomson," her son interrupted.

"Whit's it aboot?"

"I'll no' tell till I recite it."

"Recite it then."

Macgregor put his hands behind his back and, after several false starts and giggles, delivered the following:

> "Yin, twa, three!
> My mither catched a flea!
> We roastit it, an' toastit it,
> An' had it to wur tea!"

"That's a' I ken," he concluded, bursting out laughing.

His grandparents and his father laughed too, and Lizzie would have joined them had it not been for Aunt Purdie.

With a face of disgust, that lady, holding up her hands, exclaimed: "Sich vulgarity!"

Lizzie appeared to swallow something before she quietly

said: "Micht I be as bold as to speir, Mrs Purdie, if ye refer to ma son, Macgreegor, or to the words o' the pome he recitet the noo?"

"T—to the words, of course, Mrs Robison," returned Aunt Purdie hastily.

"That's a' richt, Mrs Purdie," Lizzie said, with disagreeable pleasantness. "I'm gled to hear ye referred to the words. H'm! Ay!"

Aunt Purdie opened her mouth, but fortunately the arrival of her husband just then prevented her speaking.

Robert Purdie was a big, genial man, and he had Macgregor up on his shoulder before he had been in the room a minute. The boy loved his uncle, and always associated him with large bags of what are known to some people as "hair-oil" mixtures — softish sweets with pleasing flavours, reminiscent of a barber's saloon.

"Ha'e ye been behavin' yersel', Macgreegor?" inquired Uncle Purdie presently.

"Ay," replied the youngster, while his aunt glowered.

"Aweel," said the big man, putting him gently on the floor, "awa' an' see whit ye can fin' in ma coat pooch, oot in the lobby."

With a cry of rapture Macgregor fled from the parlour. He was sampling the "poke" when his mother joined him, having announced her intention to the company of seeing if wee Jeannie slept. "Dearie, ye're no' to say thon again," she said.

"Whit, Maw?"

"Thon pome, dearie."

"Whit wey, Maw?"

"Jist because I dinna want ye to say't."

"Weel, I'll no'," replied Macgregor, with his mouth full.

"That's ma ain laddie."

"Maw, d'ye ken whit I wud like to gi'e Aunt Purdie?"

"A pickle sweeties," suggested Lizzie, trying to smile.

"Naw. I wud like to gi'e her a daud on the neb twicet!"

XIII

AN EXPERIMENT

"An' a' ye've got to dae," said Lizzie, laying the *Fireside Companion* in her lap and beginning another spell of knitting, "is jist to licht the wee stove, an' the eggs hatches theirsel's. Maist extraornar', is't no', John?"

"Dod, ay," returned John. "Whit did ye say they ca'ed it, wumman? Cremation o' chickens? Eh?"

"Incubation, John," his wife replied, after a glance at the page. "It's the het that gars the chickens come oot."

"Whit wey dae the tewkies no' come oot when ye bile the eggs, Paw?" inquired Macgregor, quitting the square blocks of wood with which he had been building "wee hooses" on the kitchen floor, and advancing to his father's knee.

"Speir at yer Maw, Macgreegor," said John, laughing. "Ye're the lad fur questions!"

"Maw, whit wey——"

"I'm thinkin' it's aboot time ye wis in yer bed, dearie," his mother observed.

"But whit wey dae the tewkies no' come oot?"

"Aweel, ye see, if they wis comin' oot then they wud shin be droondit," she said hastily. "Gi'e yer Paw a kiss noo, an'——'

"Ay, but whit wey——"

"Bilin' watter wud be ower muckle het fur the puir wee tewkies," she added, seeing that the boy was persistent. "Ye've got to gar the wee tewkies think the auld hen's settin' on them, dearie."

"If I wis to pit an egg on the hob, wud a wee tewky come oot, Maw?"

"Na, na! That wud shin roast it. Ye've got to keep it

93

nice an' cosy, but no' ower warm; jist like yersel' when ye're in yer bed. D'ye see?"

"Ay, Maw. . . . But I'm no' wearit yet."

"Let him bide a wee, Lizzie," said the indulgent John. "Did ye ever hear tell," he went on, with a twinkle in his eye, "o' the hen that fun' an aix an' sat on it fur a fortnicht, trying fur to hatchet?"

"Hoots!" murmured his wife, smiling to please him.

"Did the hen no' cut itsel', Paw?" asked his son gravely.

"Dod, I never thocht o' that, Macgreegor," his father answered, grinning.

"It was a daft kin' o' hen onywey," said the boy scornfully.

"Aw, it jist done it fur a bawr," said John, by way of apology.

"Noo, Macgreegor, yer time's up," his mother remarked, with a shake of her head.

"I'm no wearit, Maw."

"Are ye no'? An whit wey wis ye yawnin' the noo, ma mannie?"

"I wisna yawnin'."

"Whit wis ye daein' then?"

"I—I wis jist openin' ma mooth, Maw."

"Och, awa' wi' ye, laddie! Jist openin' yer mooth, wis ye? Deed, yer een's jist like twa beads wi' sleep! I seen ye rubbin' them fur the last hauf-'oor. Ay, fine ye ken it's Wee Wullie Winkie, ma dearie."

"Aw, Lizzie, the wean's fine," put in John, as he cut himself a fresh fill of tobacco. "Come here, Macgreegor, an' get a wee cuddle afore ye gang to yer bed."

"Na," said Lizzie firmly. "He'll gang to sleep on yer knee, an' then I'll ha'e a nice job gettin' him to his bed. Here, Macgreegor, till I tak' aff yer collar. . . . Noo, see if ye can louse yer buits. . . . Mercy me! if that's no' anither hole in yer stockin'. Luk at his heel, John! Ye're jist a pair, the twa o' ye! Ye're baith that sair on yer stockin's. If it's no' the heels it's the taes, an' if it's no the taes it's the soles, an' if it's no' the soles it's—— Aweel I've darned them afore, an' I daursay I'll darn them again,' she concluded, with a philosophic smile, and stooped to assist Macgregor, who was struggling with a complicated knot in the lace of his second boot.

.   .   .   .

"John," said Lizzie two mornings later—it happened to be Sunday—"I canna get Macgreegor to rise. He's sayin' he's no' weel."

"Eh!" exclaimed her husband, laying down his razor. "No' weel? I maun see——"

"No' the noo, John. I think he's sleepin' again. But —but wis ye gi'ein' him ony sweeties when ye tuk him ootbye yesterday efternune?"

"Naw, Lizzie. Ye seen a' he got yersel'. Jist thon wee bit taiblet. Is he feelin' seeck?"

"He said he wisna seeck, but jist no' weel. He's no' ill-like, but I'm no' easy in ma mind aboot him."

"I—I gi'ed him a penny yesterday," said her husband after an awkward pause.

"Aw, John!"

"But he said he wudna spend it on sweeties—an' I'm shair he didna."

"Maybe he bocht pastry. Whit fur did ye gi'e him the penny?"

"He askit fur it. Maybe he's jist a wee thing wearit, Lizzie."

Mrs Robinson shook her head, and opened a cupboard door.

"Are ye gaun to gi'e him ile?" asked John.

"Ay, when he's wauken. Oh, John, John, ye sud be mair discreet, an' no' gi'e Macgreegor a' he asks fur. But get yer shavin' dune, an' come to yer breakfast. Ye didna see wee Jeannie's flannen petticoat, did ye? Her rid yin, ye ken? I canna lay ma haun' on it, an' I'm shair it was aside her ither claes when we gaed to wur beds."

"Naw, I didna see it," John replied dully, and sadly resumed his shaving.

"It's maist aggravatin'," murmured Lizzie. "I doot I'm lossin' ma mem'ry. . . . Did ma doo no' get on her braw new flannen petticoat?" she inquired of her daughter, who, however, appeared quite happy in her old garment, sitting on a hassock and piping on a horn spoon which had a whistle in its handle. "Wee Jeannie's breid an' mulk's near ready noo," she added, whereupon wee Jeannie piped with more zest than ever.

After breakfast Lizzie interviewed her son, who was again awake.

"Are ye feelin' better noo, dearie?"

"Naw."

"Whit's like the maitter?"

"I dinna ken. I dinna want to rise, Maw."

Lizzie refrained from referring to the penny that had done the harm. "I doot ye're needin' a taste o' ile," she said.

Macgregor kept a meek silence.

"I'll gi'e ye a wee taste, an' then ye'll maybe try an' tak' yer breakfast."

"I'll try, Maw."

He took the dose like a hero, and afterwards made a meal the heartiness of which rather puzzled his mother. Then he said he was going to have another sleep.

"John," said Lizzie, "I canna think whit's wrang wi' Macgreegor. He's baith hungry an' sleepy. I wisht I kent whit he bocht wi' yer penny. I'm feart it wis some kin' o' pooshonous thing. I think I'll gang ower to Mrs Thomson an' speir if Wullie's a' richt. Wullie an' Macgreegor wis oot thegither last nicht."

"Ay," said John. "Maybe he got somethin' to eat frae Wullie."

"Maybe, John. . . . If Macgreegor's wauken when I'm awa', ye micht get him to tell ye whit he done wi' the penny. D'ye see?"

"Ay. . . . I'm rale vexed aboot the penny, wumman."

"Weel, dearie, ye maun try an' be mair discreet. Ye canna expec' a wean to be fu' o' wisdom, as Solyman says."

Left to himself—Lizzie had taken wee Jeannie with her—

John went over to the bed and gazed anxiously upon his son. Presently the boy opened his eyes.

"Weel, ma wee man," said John, with an effort to speak cheerfully, "are ye fur risin' noo?"

"Naw."

"Are ye no' ony better?"

Macgregor languidly signified that he was not.

John cleared his throat. "Whit did ye dae wi' the penny I gi'ed ye?" he asked gently.

"I spent it."

"Ay. But whit did ye spend it on? Pastry?"

"Naw."

John felt somewhat relieved. "Aweel, tell me whit ye bocht."

"I—I'll tell ye anither time, Paw," said Macgregor, after considerable hesitation.

"Did ye get ony sweeties efter yer taiblet yesterday?"

"Naw. . . . Can I get a wee tate taiblet noo, Paw?"

"Deed, I doot ye canna. Ye're no' weel."

"Ah, but I'm no' that kin' o' no' weel, Paw."

John shook his head sadly, and there ensued a long silence.

"Paw," said Macgregor at last, "hoo lang dae wee tewkies tak' to come oot their eggs?"

"Eh?"

The youngster's face was flushed as he repeated the question.

"I'm no' jist shair, Macgreegor," said John; "but I think the paper yer Maw wis readin' said it wis twa-three weeks."

"Oh!" cried Macgregor in such a tone of dismay that his father was startled.

"Whit's wrang, Macgreegor?"

"I think I'll rise noo, Paw," the boy remarked soberly.

"Are ye feelin' better?"

"Ay, I'm better."

"Whit's vexin' ye, ma wee man?" cried John suddenly, and with great tenderness.

Macgregor gave a small sniff and a big swallow as his

G

father's arm went round him. "I—I thocht the—the wee tewky wud come oot shin," he murmured brokenly.

"The wee tewky?"

"Ay. But I—I canna bide in ma b—b—bed twa-three weeks." And then from under the clothes Macgregor cautiously drew a tiny red flannel garment, which he unrolled and laid bare a hen's egg. "I gi'ed ma penny fur it, Paw. The grocer tell't me there wis nae tewky in it, but—but I thocht there wis, an' I wis wantin' to—to keep it cosy, an'—an'——"

"Aw, wee Macgregor!" exclaimed John, realizing it all, but not even smiling.

.   .   .   .

When Lizzie returned and heard the tale she was sympathetic, but not sentimental.

"I'll jist bile the egg fur yer tea, dearie," she said.

"I wud like it fried, Maw."

XIV

CONCERNING A "GUID TEAPOT"

"MACGREEGOR," said his mother, pausing in her occupation of removing the remains of the evening meal from the kitchen table, "Macgreegor, dae ye no' hear me speakin' to ye?"

"Ay, Maw," replied the boy absently.

"Weel, ye sud answer quick when I speak to ye. I want ye to—— Tits, laddie! can ye no' pey attention? Come awa' frae the jaw-box this meenit!"

"I'm jist comin', Maw."

Two minutes passed.

"Macgreegor, if ye dinna quit playin' wi' thae daft-like boats, I'll——"

"Aw, the wean's fine," interposed John, who was sitting at the fire in his shirt-sleeves, with wee Jeannie on his knee.

Lizzie paid no heed to her husband's observation. "Noo, Macgreegor," she said warningly, "I'm no' gaun to speak again. Quit thae daft-like boats, an'——"

"They're no' daft-like boats. Grandpaw made them," returned her son, as he removed the paper craft from the water, and dried his hands on his breeches.

"Aweel, yer Granpaw didna intend them fur to keep ye frae daein' whit yer Maw tell't ye."

"Paw said I wis to get sailin' them in the jaw-box."

"Ach, laddie, haud yer tongue! Ye can sail yer boats anither time."

"But Paw said I wis to get sailin' them the nicht."

"Weel, ye've got sailin' them."

"Ay, but Paw said I wis to get sailin' them fur a lang whiley the nicht, Maw."

"Mercy me! Wis there ever sic a wean?" sighed Lizzie, half to herself and half to her husband. "He wud argie-bargie wi' Solyman hissel'!"

"Maw," said Macgregor, after he had carefully dried his gaudily coloured paper boats and laid them on the dresser, "Maw, whit am I to dae?"

"Pit on yer bunnet an' yer gravat, Macgregor, an' rin roon' to Mrs M'Ostrich an' speir if she's feenished wi' the teapot she got the len' o' on Wensday."

"Dod, wumman," put in John, "ha'e ye been lendin' to Mrs M'Ostrich again?"

"Ay, John. It's no' easy to refuse, ye ken. An' the puir buddy's that fond o' comp'ny, an' she hasna muckle in her hoose."

"Ye're a rale nice wumman, Lizzie," observed John, with an affectionate grin. "I doot ye're ower guid to ither folk."

"Havers, John! But I'm no jist easy in ma mind aboot the teapot. Mrs M'Ostrich said she wantit it fur Wensday nicht—she wis ha'ein' whit she ca'ed a sma' selec' pairty—an' noo it's Monday, an'——"

"Och, dinna fash yersel', dearie."

"But it wis a rale braw teapot, John, an' ye ken I got it

frae yer mither when we wis mairrit. I mind fine hoo prood——"

"Maw, I'm ready noo," said Macgregor, interrupting what might have proved a lengthy, if not an interesting reminiscence.

Lizzie caught her son as he was leaving the kitchen. "Whaur's yer gravat, Macgreegor? Did I no' tell ye to pit on yer gravat?"

"I dinna need ma gravat," replied Macgregor, a trifle ungraciously.

"I ken faur better nor you whit ye need," said Lizzie, winding a huge red woollen comforter round his neck.

Macgregor made a face. "I dinna like that gravat. The ooss is awfu' kitly."

"Toots, laddie! Ye micht be vera thenkfu' ye've got sic a braw gravat to keep oot the cauld. Noo, aff ye gang, dearie, an' see an' no' pit aff yer time on the road. D'ye mind yer message to Mrs M'Ostrich?"

"Ay, Maw. I'm to tell her ye're feart she's broke the teapot, an'——"

"Na, na! Ye're no' to say that!" cried Lizzie hastily, while John burst out laughing. "Ye're to gi'e her ma respec's, an' tell her I wud be much obleeged fur the teapot, if she's quite feenished wi' 't. An' ye're to ask her to row it in a wheen papers, so as ye'll no' hurt it when ye're bringin' it hame. Noo, dae ye unnerstaun', dearie?"

"Ay, Maw. Wull I get sailin' ma wee boats when I come back?"

"Deed, ay! I'll get the dishes washed the noo, an' ye'll get the jaw-box to yersel'," his mother pleasantly replied.

"An' I'll mind yer boats, Macgreegor," said his father; "an' I'll mak' a mast an' sails fur yin o' them as shin as wee Jeannie gangs to her beddy-baw."

Macgregor grinned his acknowledgments to both, and with a merry heart departed upon his errand.

It was not many minutes' walk—or, in Macgregor's case, run—to the abode of Mrs M'Ostrich, but just as he reached the close-mouth he was greeted by his chum Willie Thomson.

"Whaur are ye gaun?" inquired Willie.

"I'm gaun a message to Mrs M'Ostrich," returned Macgregor.

"Whit fur?"

"Wur guid teapot."

"Weel, I'll wait on ye," said Willie, squatting himself at the foot of the stair.

Macgregor ascended, and presently the door was opened to him by Mrs M'Ostrich herself.

"Oh, it's you!" she exclaimed, not looking particularly gratified at his appearance. "Ha'e ye come fur yer Maw's teapot?"

"Ay. She was feart—naw, she wisna feart, but she said I wis to get it if ye wis feenished wi 't. An' ye wis to row it in paper."

"Come ben," said Mrs M'Ostrich, and led the way to her little parlour, which, being at the moment without any borrowed decorations, looked decidedly bare, and felt extremely chilly. "Sit ye doon, an' I'll bring yer Maw's teapot," said Mrs M'Ostrich, lighting a very modest peep of gas.

Macgregor sat down on the edge of the horsehair sofa, and the lady retired to the kitchen.

"Did ye get the stroop o' Mrs Robison's teapot mendit?" she whispered to her husband, who was drowsing before the fire.

"Ay," sleepily replied Mr M'Ostrich. "I got it mendit a' richt, but efter it wis mendit it cam' aff in ma haun'."

"Oh, dearie me! Did ever a wumman ha'e sic a sumph o' a man?" groaned Mrs M'Ostrich. "Efter it wis mendit a' richt it cam' aff in yer haun', did it? An' when I wis gaun oot fur a pair o' kippers an' a tate cheese, ye said ye wud ha'e the teapot as guid as new afore I cam' back. An' I'm no back hauf a meenit afore Mrs Robison's laddie comes to the door, wantin' the teapot, an' then I come to you fur't, an' ye tell me ye got it mendit a' richt, but the stroop cam'

aff in yer haun'! Oh, dearie me! Oh, dearie me! An'
ye sit there hauf-sleepin', ye muckle lump o'—o'——"

"I'm that wearit, wumman," said Mr M'Ostrich
plaintively. "Jist tell the laddie to say to his mither ye're
unco vexed, but ye cudna help the accident."

"That wud be a fine-like story, unless ye're gaun to
pey fur a new teapot."

"I'm no' jist daft! If folk likes to len' their cheeny to
ither folk, it's their ain fau't if it gets broke."

Mrs M'Ostrich emitted a series of impatient and angry
sounds; then, partly recovering herself, she demanded:
"Whit did ye stick on the stroop wi'?"

"Weel, I cudna fin' onythin' in the hoose but ham-fat an'
sope," said Mr M'Ostrich. "The ham-fat wudna haud, but
the sope wis a' richt—if ye didna tich the stroop efter it
wis on."

"Oh, dearie me! An' whaur did ye pit the teapot?"

"In the press. Hech, sirs, but I'm that wearit!" sighed
Mr M'Ostrich, with a huge yawn.

"Ye're jist a muckle auld tawpy!" muttered his wife, as
she took the teapot with the severed spout and laid them
on the dresser. "An' ye've jaupit them a' ower wi' ham-fat
an' sope! Oh, dearie me!"

She washed and dried the pot and spout carefully, and
after much trouble succeeded in making a parcel of them,
with the spout in, or nearly in, its proper position.

With an angry glance at her husband, who had dropped
into a peaceful doze, she left the kitchen, and delivered the
parcel to Macgregor, who was finding the parlour an
uncommonly dull place.

"Tell yer Maw I'm much obleeged fur the len' o' her
guid teapot, an' say I wis jist comin' roon' wi' 't masel' if she
hadna sent ye. Mind an' no' let it fa', an' dinna squeeze it
ower ticht in case ye break the stroop. An' here a penny fur
ye, an' here an aipple, dearie."

"Thenk ye kindly," said Macgregor, quite overcome by
the unexpected gifts.

"Guid nicht, dearie," said Mrs M'Ostrich affectionately,

as she opened the door. "An' be rale canny wi' yer Maw's braw teapot. She wud be sair vexed if ye broke it."

At the foot of the stair Macgregor found Willie Thomson sitting on the step, shivering, with his hands in his pockets.

"Ye've been a lang whiley," said the latter, rising. "Whit's that ye're eatin'?"

"Aipple," replied Macgregor, munching away. He drew the apple from his pocket, and, presenting it to his chum, said: "Ha'e a bite, Wullie. Mrs M'Ostrich is an awfu' kind auld wife. She ga'ed me a penny furbye."

"Gor!" exclaimed Willie, making an onslaught on the apple. "Are ye gaun to spend the penny noo?"

"Ay."

"Whit are ye gaun to buy?"

"Broken mixtures. Ye get an awfu' lot fur a penny."

"I'll come wi' ye," said Willie.

So they repaired to the sweet-shop, but changed their minds at the last moment, and bought sugar-ally, and Willie rushed home and returned with an old lemonade bottle filled with water, and they took turns in shaking up a portion of the sugar-ally with the water till the latter became brown and frothy and altogether delicious to their eyes.

"Ha'e a sook at it noo, Macgreegor, an' see if it's guid," said Willie, removing his finger from the bottle's neck and licking it.

Macgregor laid down his parcel, and applied the bottle to his lips. "Ay, it's rale guid!" he announced, gasping after a long, delightful pull. "Ha'e a sook to yersel', Wullie."

Willie, nothing loth, took his share, after which the bottle passed between them until empty.

"I'll awa' an' get mair watter," said Willie, and a few minutes later the young topers were at it again.

But all Macgregor's pleasure was abruptly killed when, on picking up his parcel, one end of it collapsed under his fingers with a slight grating sound.

"Whit's up?" exclaimed Willie.

"The—the teapot's broke," replied his friend, in an awestricken voice.

Willie felt the parcel cautiously. "Ay," he said, with a shake of his head, "the stroop's aff it."

Macgregor gave a sniff of despair.

"Ye maun ha'e gi'ed it a kick when ye wis drinkin' the sugar-ally watter. Ye'll ha'e to tell yer Maw ye fell," said Willie, intending, no doubt, to help his chum in the difficulty.

"But I didna fa'," said Macgregor.

"Weel, whit'll ye dae?"

"I dinna ken."

There was a long silence between them. At last Willie spoke. If not strictly truthful, he was at least sympathetic. "I'm gaun to get a penny on Setturday, an' I'll gi'e ye the hauf o' 't, an' here a bit string an' a daud o' potty," he said, pressing the last two articles into Macgregor's jacket-pocket.

Macgregor was speechless, but he glanced gratefully at Willie, while two tears rolled down his cheeks.

"Wull yer Maw skelp ye?" inquired Willie gently, after another long silence.

"Naw. But—but she'll b—b—be unco vexed. I—I'm feart to tell her."

"If I wis you," said Willie slowly, "I wud gang an' tell Mrs M'Ostrich, an' get her to gang hame wi' ye."

"Ay, she's an awfu' kind auld wife," quavered Macgregor, struck by the suggestion. And a few moments later he added, "I—I think I'll jist gang to Mrs M'Ostrich."

Willie accompanied him to the close, and with a further expression of sympathy left him there, and retired to a dusky entry across the street to watch what might happen.

Very slowly, and with an occasional gulp of misery, Macgregor ascended the stairs for the second time. Yet Mrs M'Ostrich's kindness was still so warm in his heart that he was not without faith in her assistance. But when she opened the door all he could say was:

"I've broke Maw's teapot." And then he gave way to grief.

"Ye've broke yer Maw's teapot!" echoed Mrs M'Ostrich.

shield, an gi'ed the draygon a jag in its ither e'e, an' cried, 'Come oot, ye auld taurry-biler, till I ca' the heid aff ye!' Wi' that the draygon, no' likin' to be ca'ed an auld taurry-biler, let oot a roar, an' tried fur to catch the young fairmer. But it wis jist as fou's a wulk, an' hauf-blin' furbye, an' as shin as it pit its heid oot the den the young fairmer stood up on his taes an' brocht doon the sword wi' a' his micht, an' cut aff the draygon's heid, an' the draygon wis deid.   An then——"

"Wis it bleedin', Paw?" asked Macgregor eagerly.

"Dod, ay! An' then the young fairmer got hauf the king's riches an' mairrit his dochter, an' wis happy ever efter.   An' that's a' aboot the draygon."

"Tell's anither story, Paw."

John told two other stories, and at the end of the second Macgregor said:

"I liket the draygon best.   I want to be cairrit noo."

"Na, na, I daurna tak' ye oot yer bed."

"Hap me weel, an' cairry me, Paw," said the boy.

Eventually his father gave in, rolled him in a blanket, and began to pace the kitchen floor.

"Mairch!" commanded Macgregor.   "An' whustle," he added; "whustle like a baun'!"

John obligingly began to whistle *The Girl I Left Behind Me*, and marched up and down the kitchen till Macgregor expressed himself satisfied.

"Sing noo, Paw."

"Is yer heid no' bad?"

"No' as bad as it wis.   Sing, Paw!"

"Vera weel," said John, sitting down with his burden at the fireside.

"I want to see ootbye," said the burden.

So John went over to the window, and they looked into the street, where the lamps were being lit.

> "Leerie, leerie, licht the lamps,
>   Lang legs an' crookit shanks,"

sang John softly.

Then:

> "I had a little powny,
> Its name wis Dapple Grey.
> I lent it til a leddy
> To ride a mile away.
> She whuppit it, she lashed it,
> She ca'ed it through the mire—
> I'll never lend ma powny
> Fur ony leddy's hire!"

' Sing anither," said Macgregor.

> "Wee Jokey-Birdy, tol-lol-lol,
> Laid an egg on the winda-sole.
> The winda-sole begood to crack—
> Wee Jokey-Birdy roared an' grat."

"Sing anither," said Macgregor.

John sang another half-dozen rhymes, and then Macgregor expressed himself willing to leave the window for the fireside. "Sing *A Wee Bird cam'*, Paw," he murmured, putting his arm a little further round his father's neck. It was probably the old tune that appealed to the boy, for he lay very still while John hummed the verses, swaying slightly from side to side, and gently beating time with one hand on his son's shoulder.

When the song was ended there was a short silence, and then Macgregor sighed lazily: "Sing *Leerie* again, Paw."

Leerie, so far as John knew it, was a poem of two lines set to a tune made out of three notes, but he sang it over and over again, softly and soothingly:

> "Leerie, leerie, licht the lamps,
> Lang legs an' crookit shanks"—

and having repeated it perhaps thirty times, he ceased, for Macgregor had fallen asleep.

XVI

AN INVITATION

"It's frae Mistress Purdie," said Lizzie, handing the letter which she had just perused to her husband, who was reading his paper and smoking his pipe in the fullness of contentment in front of the kitchen fire.

"Dod," exclaimed John, grinning as he examined the envelope, "but yer guid-sister's gettin' up in the warl' wi' her fancy paper an' mauve ink. Whit's she writin' ye aboot?"

"Luk at the inside, an' ye'll see. I wis expectin' the letter, fur I seen her yesterday, an' she tell't me it wis comin'."

"Ye never tell't me ye seen her, Lizzie."

"Aw, weel, I wantit to let ye get a bit surprise," said Lizzie with a faint smile.

John extracted a gilt-edged card from the envelope. "Whit's a' this, whit's a' this?" he cried, staring at the card, upon which was written in bright purple the following:

> Mr and Mrs Robert Purdie
> requests the pleasure of
> Mr and Mrs Robinson's
> company for dinner on Thurs-
> day evening, 25th December,
> at 7 o'clock P.M.

John read it through aloud, and then gaped at his wife. "Weel?" said Lizzie interrogatively.

"At seeven o'clock!" muttered John feebly.

"Tits, man!" said his wife. "Can ye no' see we're askit to a Christmas dinner?"

"Oh, that's it, is't?" And John burst into a great guffaw.

"I dinna see muckle to lauch aboot," his wife said a little impatiently.

"It's a serious maitter, nae doot," returned John, continuing his laughter. "You an' me, wumman, askit to a Christmas dinner! Haw, haw, haw! An' yer guid-sister wis tellin' ye a' aboot it, wis she?"

"Ay," said Lizzie shortly.

"Weel, tell us whit she said. Dod, but her an' her man are the gentry noo! No' but whit it wisna unco kind o' them to ask us yins to their pairty. But I doot we'll no' be able to eat muckle sae shin efter wur tea."

"Aw, we'll jist miss wur tea that nicht, John," said Lizzie, recovering her good humour. "Fur Mistress Purdie tell't me she wis gaun to gi'e us a graun' dinner—soup, an' a turkey wi' sassingers roon' aboot, an' ploom puddin', an' pies, an' frit furbye."

"I'm thinkin' ye wud be as weel to get a botle o' yer ile ready fur me, Lizzie, for this day week," he observed jocularly. "But whit wey is yer guid-sister no' ha'ein' her pairty at Ne'erday?"

"Aweel, John, she thinks it's mair genteel-like to haud Christmas. As ye ken, I'm no' jist in love wi' ma guid-sister, but Rubbert has aye been a rale kind brither, an' I wudna like to refuse to gang to the pairty. An' I'm rale gled ye're pleased aboot it."

"I didna say I wis pleased aboot it, wumman, fur I'm no' up to gentry weys," said John seriously. Then he suddenly brightened as his son entered the kitchen. "Here he comes wi' as mony feet 's a hen!" he cried merrily. "Come awa', Macgreegor, an' gi'e's yer crack. Hoo's Wullie the nicht?"

"Fine," returned Macgregor. "Wullie's maw bakit tawtie scones fur wur tea."

"Did she that? Aweel, ye'll be gettin' mair nor scones this time next week, ma mannie! Ye'll be gettin' turkeys, an' pies, an' sassingers, an' terts, an' orangers, an'——"

"Whisht, man, whisht!" cried Lizzie in dire dismay.

"Och, it's nae hairm tellin' Macgreegor aboot the guid things he'll be gettin' at his Aunt——"

"Is't a pairty, Paw?" asked Macgregor delightedly.

"Deed, ay! Yer Aunt Purdie's gaun to dae the thing in style! It's to be a rale high-class Christmas denner! Whit think ye o' that?"

Lizzie groaned helplessly.

"I like ma Uncle Purdie awfu' weel," observed Macgregor, "an' I like sassingers an' terts furbye."

"John, John!" broke out the unhappy Lizzie. "Ye've done it noo!"

"Whit ha'e I done, dearie?" her husband asked in amazement.

"I'll tell ye efter. But, fur mercy's sake, dinna cheep anither word aboot the pairty the noo."

"Vera weel, wumman," said John, in a state of complete bewilderment.

"Is turkeys guid fur eatin', Paw?" inquired Macgregor, whose vision of future delicacies prevented him noting the disturbed condition of his parents.

"Aw, it's no' bad. I tastit a turkey yinst, an' I liket it weel enough. But we'll no' heed aboot turkey the noo. Yer Maw's feart ye'll dream aboot bubbly-jocks an' sassingers till ye think ye've ett dizzens, an' then she'll be fur gi'ein' ye ile." John patted his son's head, and tried to laugh, but failed.

"I'm awfu' gled we're gaun to the pairty," said Macgregor.

"Ay, ay," said his father. "But keep quate fur a wee, an' I'll tell ye a story."

The story was of sufficient interest to keep the youngster from the tabooed subject till bedtime, but when his mother was tucking him in he murmured sleepily:

"I—I'll behave masel' awfu' weel at Aunt Purdie's pairty, Maw."

"Aw, wee Macgreegor!" whispered Lizzie, checking a sigh, as she patted and kissed him.

H

With a lump in her throat she returned to her husband, and regarded him reproachfully.

"John, John," she said at last. "Wull ye never be discreet? Ye kent fine Macgreegor canna gang to the pairty."

"No' gang to the pairty?" He sat up, staring at her. "Whit fur no'?"

"Jist because he wisna askit."

"But—but Macgreegor likes pairties!"

"Ay; that's a' richt. But I tell ye, Macgreegor wisna askit."

John's countenance turned very red. "An' whit wey wis he no' askit?" he demanded, almost fiercely.

"Oh, man, man, it's no' the thing fur a wean ava. An' supposin' Macgreegor had been askit, I wud be gey sweirt to let him gang. But noo I dinna ken whit to dae. Ye've tell't the wean he's to gang, an'—an' he canna gang."

"Ach, he can gang fine, Lizzie. He'll no' eat that muckle, an' shairly yer guid-sister can mak' room fur a wee yin. Ye can easy tell her we're bringin' Macgreegor."

"Wud ye ha'e me affrontit, John?" cried Lizzie.

"Toots, havers! She kens fine, onywey, we wudna gang wantin' Macgreegor. Deed, ay!" he added, struck by a happy thought, "that'll be the reason she didna fash to write his name on the caird. She jist kent we wud bring him. Ye needna be disturbin' yersel', dearie."

Lizzie shook her head mournfully. "They tell me ye're unco smairt at yer wark, John, an' maybe that's enough for a man; but—but—aweel, I daursay ye dae yer best." She heaved a great sigh and took up her knitting.

A minute passed ere John said slowly: "Did yer guid-sister say we *wisna* to bring Macgreegor?"

After some hesitation Lizzie replied: "She jist said she supposed we wudna be feart to leave him in the hoose that nicht, an' I tell't her I had nae doot I wud get Mistress M'Faurlan to bide wi' him an' wee Jeannie till we got hame."

"Aw, I see. . . . I see," said John thoughtfully. "She

supposed we wudna be feart to leave him in the hoose, did she suppose?" And suddenly his wrath got the better of him. "I tell ye whit it is, wumman," he cried, "she didna want Macgreegor!"

"Tits! Ye needna flee up like that, John," said his wife. "Ye're fair rideec'lous aboot Macgreegor. Whit wud ye say if I wis to tak' the huff because wee Jeannie wisna askit?"

"Wee Jeannie's no' heedin' aboot pairties. There's time enough fur her. . . . There's time enough fur you to tak' the huff, as ye ca' it, wife, when she likes pairties an' disna get askit. . . . Ye needna say anither word, Lizzie. . . . I'll no' pit a foot inside yer guid-sister's door fur a' the turkeys, an' sassingers, an' snashters in creation! I'm jist tellin' ye!" And John rose abruptly, caught up his cap, and stalked from the kitchen and out of the house.

When he returned, half-an-hour later, he was calm, but absolutely firm in his determination not to be present at the Purdies' Christmas dinner.

"Them as disna want Macgreegor disna want me," he said, in reply to Lizzie's pleadings.

"My! but ye're a dour yin!" she said at last. "Hoo dae ye ken Mistress Purdie disna want Macgreegor?"

"She aye had a spite at the wean; an' fine ye ken it!" he retorted.

Lizzie wavered. She knew the aunt and nephew had never got on comfortably, yet she was anxious to keep on friendly terms with the former for her brother's sake.

"I wudna ha'e let Macgreegor gang, even if he had been askit," she said, after a pause. "He's ower young, an' he needs haudin' doon instead o' bein' pit furrit afore his elders. But—but I'm vexed—oh, John, I'm vexed fur the wean, fur he'll be that disappintit. Oh, I wisht ye hadna said onythin' aboot the pairty."

"'Deed, Lizzie, I wisht I hadna," admitted John despondently. "But, ye see, I thocht the wean——"

"Ye'll jist ha'e to tell him we're no' gaun to the pairty efter a'," said Lizzie.

"Wud ye no' gang yersel', dearie?"

"John!"

"Weel, I thocht ye wis set on the pairty."

"Ach, John, ye ken fine I thocht you wud like it. . . . Sirs, the day! it's an unco peety! . . . But I'm rale gled I didna tell Mrs Purdie we wud gang fur certain."

"Ye're a wice wumman!" said her husband admiringly.

"I'll jist ha'e to tell her we canna gang. But whit aboot Macgreegor? Wull *you* tell him, John?"

"Na, na!   Never let bug to Macgreegor there's to be nae pairty till I can mak' up some ither treat fur him," said John, beginning to recover his spirits.

"Whit kin o' a treat?"

"Och, I'll tell ye when I get it a' arranged."

"Ah, but, John, ye're no' to gang an' be wasterfu'," said Lizzie warningly.   "Wud it no' be best jist to tell him he'll get his treat at Ne'erday?"

"I'll see, I'll see,'" replied her husband.   "But never let bug aboot the pairty till I tell ye.   Promise, dearie."

Lizzie promised reluctantly, and John lit his pipe, which had been cold for some time, and smoked steadily for the next ten minutes without speaking a word.

"But whit am I to write to Mistress Purdie?" inquired Lizzie ere she slept that night."

"Oh," said her husband with a chuckle, "jist say we're vexed we canna gang to her pairty, because Macgreegor's ha'ein' a pairty o' his ain that night."

"Ma word, John!" said Lizzie, and proceeded to ask questions to which she got no answers.

.   .   .   .   .

The next day, Friday, John was exceedingly thoughtful.

On Saturday he was grave; on Sunday he was unusually glum.   On Monday he was distinctly irritable and nervous; and on Tuesday he was wrapped in gloom.

But on Wednesday he came home to his dinner in a state of repressed excitement, and his wife made many inquiries without receiving any satisfaction.   At tea he burst out into frequent guffaws without apparent reason.

hastened after Macgregor, crying: "I'll gi'e ye the ticket, I'll gi'e ye the ticket!"

"Wull ye?" said his friend, halting.

"Ay. But—but I'll no' try to get in to the surree."

"Whit?"

"I'll let ye gang in instead o' me."

"Nae fears! I wudna dae that, Wullie. No' likely!"

"Wud ye no' gang in wi'oot me?"

"Awa' an' bile yer heid! As if I wud gang in wi'oot ye! Jist you gi'e me the ticket an' come to the door efter me, an' I'll shin get ye in. An' if they'll no' let ye in, I'll gi'e ye back yer ticket, an' I'll gang awa' hame."

The ticket being transferred, they approached the entrance to the hall of happiness.

"Wullie," said Macgregor in a whisper, "can ye no' greet?"

"Whit wey?"

"To mak' the beadle vexed fur ye because ye've lost yer ticket. Ye see? . . . Try an' greet, Wullie."

"I canna," said Willie despairingly. "I'm ower big to greet."

"Weel, try an' luk awfu' meeserable."

Through sheer nervousness Willie succeeded in doing so, and they climbed the few steps to the doorway, where the church officer had taken his stand.

Macgregor held out the ticket, and carelessly pointing to his friend, who looked like running away, remarked:

"This yin's lost his ticket."

"Eh?" said the beadle.

"I'm sayin' he's lost his ticket."

"Whaur did he loss it?"

"Ootbye."

"Mphm. He's no' the first yin that's lost his ticket the nicht," the beadle observed severely. "What's yer name?" he demanded of Willie.

"Wullie Thomson."

"Who's yer teacher?"

"Maister M'Culloch."

The beadle passed in several children who presented their tickets, and then, opening the swing-doors, bawled across the hall: "Maister M'Culloch, ye're wantit, please."

"I'll wait fur ye inside, Wullie," hurriedly whispered Macgregor, afraid of meeting the young man who was his teacher as well as Willie's.

"But—but if he winna let me in?" said Willie.

"If he winna let ye in, I'll come oot again. Ye needna be feart, Wullie." And Macgregor disappeared through the swing-doors.

Two minutes later he was joined by his chum.

"I kent ye wud get in," said Macgregor.

"Ay," said Willie, adding, "but *you*'re nickit, Macgreegor."

"Did he see me?"

"Ay; he seen ye!"

"Is he gaun to pit me oot?"

"I dinna ken. He jist askit me whit wey ye didna wait ootside fur me. But he wis rale nice. He wisna angry at me fur gi'ein'—I mean, fur lossin'—ma ticket."

"Wis he no'? Come awa' this wey, Wullie. I'm no' wantin' him to catch me."

"Maybe he wudna pit ye oot," said Willie, following his friend. "He's rale kind. D'ye mind when ye fell in the glaur, an' he cleaned yer face wi' his guid hanky?"

"Ay. But I'm no' wantin' him to speak to me the nicht. We'll get a sate at the back thonder."

"But we'll no' see the magyic lantern an' the con*joo*rer as weel there," the other objected.

"We'll gang furrit when they screw doon the lichts fur the lantern. Come on! There a man gi'ein' oot the pokes, an' thonder anither comin' wi' the tea."

"Haud yer tongue," said a little girl beside them; "the meenister's gaun to ask a blessin'."

"Aw, *you*'re here, Maggie, are ye?" retorted Macgregor as jauntily as possible, recognizing a dweller in his own street, who usually saluted him by putting out her tongue.

"Ay, it's jist me. Hoo did ye get in, Macgreegor?"

she inquired, with an unpleasant grin, immediately the brief grace was finished.

"Through the door," replied Macgregor smartly.

"An' ye'll gang oot through the door gey shin," Maggie exclaimed unkindly. "I ken fine ye had nae ticket. Ye're jist a cheat! An' cheatery'll choke ye!"

Fortunately most of the youngsters were already being served with tea and bags of buns, otherwise more heads would have turned in Macgregor's direction.

"If ye wisna a lassie, I wud knock the face aff ye!" the boy muttered wildly. "I'm no' a cheat!"

"I ken ye're no' a cheat, Macgreegor," said the small voice of another little girl.

"Ye dinna ken him, Katie," said Maggie sharply.

"Ay; I ken him. He wudna be a cheat," returned Katie gently, with a shy glance at her hero.

But Willie was dragging his friend away to another part of the hall, and the latter took no notice of his girl champion. Perhaps he was feeling ashamed.

Twenty minutes later Willie genially observed: "I've ett mair nor you, Macgreegor."

"Ye've a bigger mooth," returned Macgregor sulkily. He felt that nearly everyone was watching him, and Maggie's words rankled.

After tea the minister delivered a very brief address on Honesty and Truth, and the youngster, though he assumed his most unrepentant expression, trembled inwardly, and was glad when the speaker finished. Then came the conjurer, but it was not until the lights were lowered for the magic-lantern item of the entertainment that Macgregor began to feel free to take his pleasure with the other children.

"We'll gang furrit noo," he whispered to Willie, and in the dim light the twain crept forward and crushed themselves into a seat well in front, much to the indignation of its occupants. Indeed, a disturbance seemed inevitable, when happily the operator uncapped the lantern, and the first picture shone upon the screen.

"If ye kick me again," said Macgregor, hoarsely, to the boy next him, "I'll gi'e ye a shot on the nose!"

"Keep quiet, Macgregor," said a voice from the bench behind, and the voice was that of Mr M'Culloch, his teacher.

Macgregor kept *very* quiet throughout the lantern exhibition.

.   .   .   .

As the children departed from the hall, each received a bag of sweets and shook hands with the minister and also with his or her teacher.

For a moment Macgregor was tempted to make a bolt for freedom, but his courage prevailed, and, after receiving his sweets, he kept his place in the line of boys and girls that filed slowly towards the door. And—strange thing!—he received as kindly a look and handshake from the minister as did any of the other scholars. So surprised was he that he dropped the sweets, and lost his place in the line, having to stand aside till all had passed. And then he found himself shaking hands with the minister a second time.

A nasty choky feeling came in his throat as he approached his teacher. Where was the latter's severe and vengeful look?

"Well, Macgregor," said Mr M'Culloch ever so kindly, laying a light hand on the boy's shoulder.

Macgregor gave a queer, gulping sound. "I'm no' wantin' the sweeties!" he cried, and, shoving the bag into the teacher's hand, he rushed from the hall.

Willie was waiting for him in the street. "Did ye catch it frae Maister M'Culloch?" he inquired.

"Naw," said Macgregor sharply.

They walked some distance in silence, Willie observing that his chum was in trouble, but knowing from experience that the latter was not always grateful for unsolicited sympathy.

But at last Willie said in a shamed manner: "I—I think I'll no' buy sweeties again wi' ma heathen mishnary boax bawbee."

The other made no remark, and there was another long silence broken again by Willie.

"Are ye gaun to the schule next Sawbath?" he asked timidly.

"I'll see."

This was not encouraging, so Willie changed the subject, by starting a rather one-sided discussion on the conjurer and the magic lantern, which was kept up till they came to the parting of their homeward ways.

"They're awfu' guid sweeties we got the nicht," remarked Willie, conveying a couple from his pocket to his mouth.

"Ay," assented Macgregor dismally, and turned abruptly away.

He walked slowly home, and when he reached the house his father was waiting for him at the door.

"Ye furgot yer sweeties at the surree, Macgreegor."

"Eh?" cried the boy, taken aback.

"Yer teacher wis here the noo an' left thur fur ye. He didna want ye to be disappintit. Ye're the lucky yin!" said his father, laughing and bringing *two* bags from behind his back.

His son smiled broadly, it might even have been virtuously.

XVIII

GRANPAW PURDIE COMES TO TEA

"Ir wud be gey cauld on the boat," said Mrs Robinson to her father, who had just arrived from Rothesay.

"It wis a' that," returned Mr Purdie. "But ye're fine an' cosy here, Lizzie. Ye ken hoo to mak' a fire," he added approvingly, stretching his hands to the blaze.

"I'm aye thenkfu' fur plenty meat an' plenty coals. I hope ye'll get as guid a fire at Rubbert's hoose. Mistress Purdie thinks mair o' her graun' freens' firesides nor her ain,

I doot." Lizzie could not resist a hit at her sister-in-law now and then.

"Och, wumman," said Mr Purdie pleasantly, "ye're no' to be ower severe on yer brither's guidwife. Ye sud try to mind she hasna got a Macgreegor an' a wee Jeannie; an' maybe that's the reason she's kin' o' daft aboot comp'ny an' pairties."

"Weel, maybe ye're richt, fayther," admitted Mrs Robinson, somewhat unwillingly. "A' the same, I'm rale gled ye cam' here fur yer tea afore ye gaed to stop wi' Mistress Purdie an' Rubbert. But wud ye no' be the better o' a taste o' speerits? John said I wis to be shair an' ha'e a dram in the hoose in case ye needit it." She produced a small bottle from the dresser drawer.

"'Deed, it wis rale kind o' John to mind an auld man. It's a guid sign when the young minds the auld, Lizzie."

"Hoots! ye're no' to talk like as if ye wis Methusalah! John didna want ye to feel ye cudna get a taste, if ye wantit it. I daursay John wud like a dram hissel' whiles, an' I wudna be interferin'; we've never even spoke aboot it; but I jist ken, since the day Macgreegor wis born, John's been teetotal, except fur maybe a gless at the New Year, an' the Fair, an' maybe a mairriage. Ay, John's a rale——"

"Ye've got a rale proper man, ma lass," observed Mr Purdie gently, as he helped himself to a drop of whisky.

"Och, John's weel enough," said Lizzie, afraid of having been sentimental.

"He's shairly late the nicht," said her father, consulting his fat silver watch.

"Aweel, ye see, fayther, he's foresman noo, an' he disna aye get awa' prompt to the meenit. Macgreegor's awa' oot to meet him. He gangs near every nicht, an' they come hame thegither, chatterin' an' lauchin' like a pair o' weans. Whiles they tell me their bit joke, but I canna say I see muckle to lauch at. Hooever, if they're pleased, I suppose that's a' aboot it."

"An' ye canna help bein' pleased yersel' if they're pleased —eh?" said the old man, chuckling. "Weel, weel, ye

wudna be yersel', ma dochter, if ye let on ye wis as pleased
as ye kent ye wis. Ye never wis the yin to mak' a hullabaloo
aboot things that pleased or hurtit ye—no' even when ye
wis a bit lassie. . . . Weel, here's ma love to you an' yer
man an' yer weans! Ye'll be a prood wumman aboot John
bein' appintit foresman. Dod, ye needna be pretendin'
ye're no'! I'm thinkin' ye'll be removin' to a bigger hoose
some fine day afore lang."

"Na!" she replied soberly. "We'll no' move fur twa
year onywey."

"Is that John's wey o' thinkin'?"

Lizzie smiled slightly. "John wis fur movin' at the term,
but I tell't him he wisna to gang an' get peery-heidit ower
his bit rise. Ye maun creep afore ye gang, as Solyman says."

"I hope ye didna vex yer man," said Mr Purdie seriously.

"Vex him? 'Deed no! But if it wisna fur me haudin'
him doon, John wudna be lang afore he wis spendin' a' he
got. He's that kind-hertit an' free, ye ken," she said, with
a touch of warmth; "but as lang as I'm spared he's no'
gaun to get wastin' his siller. . . . Whit's that ye're sayin',
duckie?" she asked wee Jeannie, who was playing about the
floor. "D'ye hear yer Paw comin'?"

"Paw and Greegy comin'," replied wee Jeannie; "comin'
wi' gundy," she added.

"Na, na, dearie; this isna gundy nicht," said her mother
gently.

"I wudna be ower shair o' that," remarked Mr Purdie.
"Come to yer granpaw, daurlin', an' ripe his pooches."

"Aw, fayther," cried Lizzie. "But wee Jeannie mauna
get ony till she's had her tea. . . . Here John and Macgreegor noo."

There was a sound of mingled laughter, and a moment
later father and son entered, to exchange hearty greetings
with Mr Purdie.

"An' hoo's ma auld freen' Macgreegor?" inquired the
old gentleman genially of his grandson, while John was
enjoying a wash, and Lizzie, having laid the tea-table, was
hastily giving her daughter a tidy-up.

"I'm fine," returned Macgregor, adding "thenk ye," as he caught a look from his mother. "Wis ye dry, Granpaw?" he asked, noticing the glass in Mr Purdie's hand.

"Haud yer tongue, an' dinna ask impiddent questions," exclaimed Lizzie, while John guffawed into the towel with which he was polishing his face.

Mr Purdie chuckled good-humouredly. "Weel, I wisna jist whit ye wud ca' dry, Macgreegor, but yer Maw thocht I wis needin' a wee drap meddicine," he replied, emptying the glass.

"It wisna ile?" began the boy. "Naw, I ken it wisna ile, fur ye wud ha'e got ile in a spune. Wis ye badly on the boat?" he inquired sympathetically. "Wis ye throwin'?"

Fortunately Lizzie did not hear, and Mr Purdie chuckled again, and explained that he had not had a rough passage, but only a very cold one.

"Wis the boat no' whumlin'?" asked the boy, obviously disappointed. "I like when the boat's whumlin' aboot. I'm no' feart. Whit kin' o' meddicine did Maw gi'e ye? Wis it unco ill to tak'?"

"'Deed, I've swallowed waur, Macgreegor."

"Did ye no' get ony carvies to pit awa' the taste? Carvies is awfu' guid efter ile."

"Na; yer Maw didna think I needit carvies. An' hoo are ye gettin' on at the schule?"

"Fine! I gi'ed Geordie M'Culloch a bashin' the day," whispered Macgregor, so that his mother should not hear.

"Ah, but ye sudna fecht," said Mr Purdie, choking back a chuckle, and looking solemn. "Ye ken the pome— 'Let dugs delight to bark an' bite——'"

"It's a daft pome! Geordie M'Culloch needit a bashin'."

"Whit wis he daein' to ye?"

"Naethin'. He's feart fur me."

"Ah, but ye sudna strike a laddie less nor yersel'."

"He's faur bigger nor me, an' he wis stealin' pincils frae the wee yins, an' I tell't him to gi'e back the pincils, an' he said he wudna, an' I bashed him, an' he gi'ed back the pincils, an' gaed awa' bummin'."

"Weel, weel. . . . An' whit aboot yer spellin'? Ye'll be able to spell lang words noo."

"I'm no' heedin' aboot spellin'."

"But ye maun pey attention to yer lessons, Macgreegor. Ye'll no' be dux, I doot, frae the wey ye speak aboot spellin'."

"Naw, I'm no' dux."

"Whaur are ye?"

"Second fit," said Macgregor, after a little hesitation.

"Ye'll no' like that?"

"Ay; I like it fine. Wullie Thomson's fit, an' him an' me likes sittin' thegither."

"But that'll never dae," said Mr Purdie; and he was about to give some kindly advice when Lizzie summoned them all to the tea-table.

"Noo, wait till yer Granpaw asks a blessin'," said Lizzie to Macgregor, who was reaching out for a slice of hot toast—the "outside" bit—which lay on the top, and which he particularly desired.

Old Mr Purdie bowed his head and murmured a simple grace, at the end of which Macgregor's eager hand went forth again.

"Pass the toast to yer Granpaw," commanded his mother.

Macgregor obeyed, but, his mother being busy with the teapot, he took the opportunity of whispering to his grandfather: "Dae ye no' like the inside best?"

"I'm no' heedin', ma mannie. Maybe the ootside's a wee thing cheuch fur ma auld grinders."

"Ay, it's awfu' cheuch," said Macgregor. "But I'll tak' it, if ye like, Granpaw." Which he did, much to the amusement of John, who had pretended not to notice anything.

.   .   .   .

"Maw! am I no' to get an egg?" said Macgregor in a hoarse undertone to his mother, as his father and grandfather chipped the tops of their eggs.

"Hoots! laddie, ye're no' needin' an egg," replied

I

Lizzie, as she stirred a hot mess of bread and milk for her daughter.

"Gi'e him an egg, Lizzie," said John.

"Tits! John," she returned.

"Whit wey can I no' get an egg, Maw?" inquired the son.

"Jist because ye're no' needin' an egg; an' there's no' anither in the hoose, onywey."

"Ha'e, Macgregor," said his father, a few seconds later, "here the tap aff mines." (It was really half the egg.)

"An' here the tap aff mines," said Mr Purdie.

With a brief acknowledgment Macgregor fell to.

"Ye jist spile the wean," said Lizzie, frowning.

"I like fried eggs better nor biled," observed the boy, when he had cleaned the shells.

Lizzie, with a great effort, restrained herself.

.   .   .   .   .   .

After tea Mr Purdie produced his offerings of sweets, and while the young folks enjoyed them the elders had an opportunity for a short "crack." When the old man said he must go, John rose to accompany him. So did Macgregor, donning his woollen muffler and bonnet in the twinkling of an eye.

"Whit are ye efter noo, Macgreegor?" inquired his mother.

"I'm gaun ootbye wi' Paw and Granpaw, Maw."

"Ye're no' gaun ower the door the nicht," said Lizzie decidedly.

John was silent, looking uncomfortable; Mr Purdie appeared to be trying to pretend he did not notice anything.

"Whit wey, Maw?" said Macgregor.

"Jist because I say ye're no' to gang," said Lizzie.

'Paw said I wud get, Maw."

"Eh? When did yer Paw say that?"

"When we wis comin' hame the nicht."

"Ay, Lizzie," put in John, "I tell't the wean he wud get oot wi' his Granpaw. An' whit fur no'?"

Lizzie ignored the appeal. "Ha'e ye learned yer spellin' fur the morn?" she demanded of her son.

"Ay."

"When did ye learn it?   No' in the hoose, I'm shair."

"Comin' hame frae the schule."

"Hoo cud you learn it comin' hame frae the schule, laddie?"

"Me an' Wullie Thomson gaed up a close, an' he heard me, an' I heard him."

"H'm!" muttered Lizzie dubiously.   "Bring yer book to me, an' I'll hear ye."

It was without much alacrity that Macgregor brought his book and showed his mother the place.

"Can ye spell 'People'? she asked.

"Ay."

"Aweel, let me hear ye spell it."

"P—E——" began the boy.

"John," said Lizzie to her husband, "it ill becomes ye to mak' faces.   Awa' oot to the stairhied an' smoke yer pipe."   And poor John, who had been trying to signal "O" to his son by lip language, reluctantly obeyed.

"Rest ye a meenit," said Lizzie to Mr Purdie, who also made to depart.   Then she resumed the lesson.   "Come awa', dearie.   Spell 'People.'"

"P—E—O—P——"

"Ay; but that's no' it a'."

"—L—E," said Macgregor at last.

"Richt!" said Lizzie.   "Spell 'Money.'"

He spelled it and the next half-dozen words correctly, though with some hesitation.

"Ye're a wee thing slow, but ye're better at the spellin' nor I thocht.   'Deed, it's the first nicht ye've been kin' o' shair o' the words.   Weel, jist yin mair; an' if ye spell it richt, ye'll gang wi' yer Granpaw.   Spell 'Receive.'"

"R—E—C——"

"Weel, whit mair?"

(At this point Mr Purdie nearly put his finger in his left eye.)

"Come awa'," said Lizzie encouragingly.   She was really quite proud of her son.

"R—E—C——IEVE," said Macgregor in a burst of triumph.

"Ye're wrang," said Lizzie sadly.

Grandfather Purdie smote his breast. "Aw! Did I tell ye wrang, ma wee man?" he cried. "I aye had a deeficulty wi' thae——" He stopped in confusion.

.   .   .   .   .   .

The most valuable variety of humour is that which enables people to laugh when they find they have been deceived—to laugh away the natural anger.

Lizzie laughed eventually, and Macgregor had his own way. But she rose half-an-hour earlier the next morning—which was pretty early—roused up her son, and drummed the spelling into him. If it hadn't been for Willie Thomson he *might* have reached the top of the class.

XIX

"ARMS AND THE BOY"

"But it wis rale kind o' Mistress Purdie to mind Macgreegor's birthday," said Mrs Robinson to her husband, who was critically examining a rather gaudily covered little book, entitled *Patient Peter; or, The Drunkard's Son.*

"Ay; it wis rale kind o' her," replied John, slowly and without much enthusiasm.

"Efter a'," she continued, endeavouring to do justice to her sister-in-law, "it's no' the present itsel' we've got to think o', but the speerit——"

"Dod, but ye're richt there, wumman! There's nae want o' speerit aboot this book," he interrupted with a dry laugh. "*Patient Peter; or, The Drunkard's Son!* That's a bonny-like book to gi'e til a wean!"

"Whisht, man!" said Lizzie, checking a smile. "Ye ken fine whit I meant. An' ye're no' to let on to Macgreegor ye dinna like it. Him an' wee Jeannie'll be in the noo."

"Dis Macgreegor like it hissel'?"

"Weel, I daursay he wud ha'e liket somethin' else, John. He wantit to gi'e it til wee Joseph, the puir laddie that's been lyin' badly sic a lang while; but, of coorse, I wudna let him."

"Wee Joseph wudna be muckle the better o' this book, I'm thinkin'. But it wis unco nice o' Macgreegor to think o' his puir wee freen'. I'll hae to gi'e him a bawbee fur that."

"Na, na, John!" cried Lizzie.

"Whit fur no', dearie? I tell ye, I like when the weans thinks o' ither weans. Ay; an' fine ye like it yersel'!"

"Ah, but ye see——"

"Aw, I ken ye think he sudna be rewardit fur bein' kind. But I'm shair he wudna expec' ony reward."

"Maybe no'. But——"

"But, a' the same, I like to encourage him."

"Ay; that's a' richt, but——"

Lizzie's remonstrance was here interrupted by the return of her son and daughter.

"Did ma doo like bein' ootbye wi' her big brither?" she cried affectionately.

"Ay, Maw, she likes it," replied Macgregor, who, occasionally, was good enough to oblige his mother by taking the toddling Jeannie for a short walk up and down the street. "But she gangs awfu' slow," he added, as he relinquished the small fingers, "an' she's aye tum'lin'."

"She'll shin be rinnin' races wi' ye, Macgreegor," said his father pleasantly.

"'Deed, ay!" said his mother. "Ye'll shin be rinnin' races wi' Greegy—eh, ma daurlin'?"

"Lassies canna rin fast," returned the boy. "Their legs is ower wake."

"I hope ye didna let yer sister fa'," his mother interposed, as she brushed a little dust from the child's lower garment.

"I canna help her coupin' whiles, Maw," said Macgregor easily. "But I aye keep a grup o' her haun', an' I never let her fa' furrit—jist backwards; an' she jist sits doon an' disna hurt hersel' ava."

"No' hurtit," observed the mite gravely.

"There, ye see!" said her brother triumphantly.

"I'm shair he aye tak's guid care o' wee Jeannie," put in John, appealing to his wife.

"I'm shair I never said he didna," rejoined Lizzie, patting her boy's shoulder.

John's face assumed an expression of complete satisfaction. "Here, Macgreegor! come ower here till I speak to ye," he cried in a pleased voice.

Macgregor obeyed willingly, while his father fumbled in a pocket.

"John," whispered Lizzie warningly.

But John smiled merrily back to her, and then turned to his son. "I wis gaun to gi'e ye a bawbee, Macgreegor, but I ha'ena yin, so here a penny instead."

"Oh, John!" murmured his wife.

"Thenk ye, Paw," said Macgregor, grinning.

"D'ye ken whit it's fur, ma mannie?"

"Naw," replied Macgregor, who had already received a bright shilling as a birthday offering from his father. (The bright shilling, however, had been promptly taken by his mother, much to his own disgust, to the Savings Bank, along with a half-crown received from Grandfather Purdie.)

"Aweel, it's fur thinkin' o' gi'ein' yer book to puir wee Joseph," said John, stroking the back of the boy's head.

"I wud like fine to gi'e it to Joseph, Paw. Maw said I wisna," said Macgregor, with a glance at his mother, whose attention was apparently entirely taken up by her daughter.

"Yer Maw thinks it's no' jist the thing to gi'e awa' a present," John explained; adding, "an' I daursay she's richt."

"Whit wey, Paw?"

"Weel, ye see, whit wud ye dae if yer Aunt Purdie cam' to the hoose an' speirt if ye liket the book, an' if ye wis keepin' it nice an' clean? Yer Maw'll ha'e to pit a cover on it fur ye. Eh, Lizzie?"

"Ay, I'll dae that," his wife answered pleasantly. She felt that, on the whole, her man was behaving really discreetly.

"But I'm no' heedin' aboot the book, Paw, an' wee Joseph likes readin'," said Macgregor. "An' it's a daft story onywey."

"Hoo can ye say that, Macgreegor, when ye've never read it?" his mother inquired.

"I've read some o' it. There's naebody gets kilt in it. I like stories aboot folk gettin' their heids cut aff, or stabbit through an' through wi' swords an' spears. An' there's nae wild beasts. I like stories aboot black men gettin' ett up, an' white men killin' lions, an' teagurs, an' bears, an'——"

"Whisht, whisht, laddie," cried Lizzie.

"Aw, the wean's fine," said John, smiling. "Dod, I doot I like thur kin' o' stories best masel'."

"But I'm no' heedin' aboot this book," Macgregor went on, regarding the volume with great contempt. "It's jist aboot a laddie ca'ed Peter, an' his Maw's deid, an' his Paw's an awfu' bad man, an' he's aye strikin' Peter an' gi'ein' him crusts to eat, an' Peter jist eats the crusts an' asks a blessin' furbye, an' in the end he gangs ootbye when it's snawin' to luk fur his Paw, an' gets drookit, an' gets the cauld in his kist, an' dees, an' his Paw gets rin ower wi' a lorry, an' dees tae; but Peter gets tooken up to the guid place, an' his Paw gets tooken doon to the——"

"Whisht, Macgreegor!" cried his mother again. "Ye're no' to——"

"It's in the book, Maw."

"Weel, weel, dearie. It's a sad story that. But ye wud be gey sair vexed fur puir Peter deein'?"

"Naw, I wisna."

"Aw, Macgreegor!" said Lizzie reproachfully, while her husband barely checked a guffaw.

"Weel, it's no' a true story, Maw."

"Hoo dae ye ken that?"

"I ken it fine."

"But mony a laddie's got nae Maw—puir thing!—an' a bad Paw, an' has to eat crusts."

"Ay; but they dinna ask a blessin' on the crusts."

John jumped up and went to the window, where he stood with his hand to his mouth and his shoulders heaving.

"I'm vexed to hear ye speakin' like that, Macgreegor," said his mother sternly.

"Whit wey, Maw?"

"Because ye sudna mak' a mock o' sic things. An' maybe the laddie in the book wis gled to get the crusts."

"But it's a' lees aboot him! I dinna believe a word!"

"Haud yer tongue, Macgreegor! That's no' the wey to speak aboot the present yer Aunt Purdie sent ye."

"But I wud rayther ha'e gotten a pistol fur firin' peas."

"Mercy me! I'm thenkfu' ye didna get *that!* Ye wud shin ha'e us a' blin'."

"I wudna fire it at ony o' you yins," he graciously returned, with a glance at his relatives.

"Na, na," said Lizzie not unkindly. "That's no' the kin' o' toy fur a laddie. An', onywey, there's nae use wishin' fur whit ye canna get, dearie. Yer Paw wudna like ye to ha'e ony kin' o' fireairms aboot ye. Wud ye, John?"

John pretended not to hear.

"He micht pit oot wee Jeannie's een in mistak'," she continued. "Every day ye read i' the papers o'——"

"I *wudna!*" exclaimed Macgregor indignantly. "Wud I, Jeannie?" he cried, appealing to his little sister.

"Ay," cheerfully assented the cherub, who had been too busy playing with some blocks of wood on the floor to pay any attention to the conversation of her elders.

"Ach! She disna ken whit she's sayin'!" exclaimed the boy in disgust.

"There's mony a true word spoken in eegnorance, as Solyman says," observed Lizzie sagely.

"I wisht I had a pistol," he muttered, as if he had not heard her.

"Weel, laddie, I've tell't ye ye canna get a pistol. Whaur wud ye get the money to buy it? Eh?"

"It wud jist cost thruppence, an' I can get the money oot the bank."

"Na, na. The money maun bide in the bank, Macgreegor."

"I dinna like ma money bidin' in the bank, Maw."

"Ye'll like it some day. . . . John, come ower here an' tell Macgreegor a story."

John left the window, but his son put on his bonnet and moved to the door.

"Whaur are ye gaun, Macgreegor?" inquired Lizzie.

"Ootbye."

"Ay; but I want to ken whaur ye're gaun."

"To see wee Joseph."

"Aw. That's a guid laddie!" said Lizzie, and John beamed approval. "But ye're no' to bide lang. An' when ye come back I'm gaun to write to yer Aunt Purdie to tell her ye like yer book."

"But I dinna like it, Maw."

Lizzie was going to speak, but John, with a laugh he could not restrain, interposed, saying: "Weel, weel, we'll see aboot the letter when Macgreegor comes back."

Macgregor returned to the table and picked up *Patient Peter*.

"Can I gi'e wee Joseph the *len'* o' ma book?"

"Dod, ay!" said John, delighted.

"'Deed, ay!" said Lizzie, also pleased. "But bide a wee, an' I'll pit a cover on it." She opened a drawer in the dresser wherein she methodically placed odds and ends, and drew forth a sheet of brown paper, in which she encased the covers of *Patient Peter*.

"That'll keep it clean," she said. "Tell wee Joseph to pit a bit paper at the place, an' no' to turn doon the pages."

"Ay, Maw," said Macgregor, and departed.

When he had been gone a couple of minutes John turned to his wife, and said diffidently: "It's a peety the wean's disappintit wi' the book."

"It is that," said Lizzie. "But it wudna dae to let him get everythin' he wants."

"But it's his birthday, wumman. . . . I—I wad like fine to gi'e him a pistol."

"Weel, I never!"

"The pistol he wants isna dangerous, Lizzie."

"I'm no' sae shair o' that!"

"It's jist like a pop-gun, ye ken."

"Is't?"

"Ay. It wudna hurt a flee."

"Flees is no' that easy hit."

John laughed heartily. "Dod, but ye had me there! . . . But wud ye no' let me buy the wean a pistol? I'll see he disna dae ony hairm. . . . 'Deed, I mind fine when I wis a wean I aye wantit a gun or a pistol."

"I dinna think it wud be wice to gi'e yin to Macgreegor. Ye never ken whit he'll dae."

"Hoots, toots! Say the word, an' I'll rin an' buy him yin, Lizzie. Thon book wisna the thing to gi'e a wean ava."

"Ye sudna say that, John. . . . But, a' the same, I dinna think it wis a vera nice book. Nae doot Mistress Purdie meant weel," she added grudgingly. . . . "Weel, John, if ye'll promise no' to let him be reckless, I'll say nae mair aboot it. . . . Awa' an' buy the pistol!"

John went without delay.

.   .   .   .

As he ascended the stairs on his return in the dusk, John heard a click, and something stung his cheek. This was followed by a badly stifled cackle of laughter, which he recognized.

"Macgreegor!" he exclaimed.

For a moment there was dead silence; then someone descended the flight of stairs above him.

"I thocht ye wis a brigand, Paw," said his son. "I didna hit ye, did I?"

"Aye, ye hut me!"

"Aw, Paw!" The regret in the boy's voice was intense. "Whaur did I hit ye?"

John put a finger to his cheek.

"I wis aimin' at yer hert," said Macgregor. "I'm gled I missed."

John wondered what *he* should say.

"I—I—I didna mean to hurt ye, Paw," murmured his son. "I—I didna mean it."

"But whit did ye hit me wi'? My! it wis gey nippy!"

"It wis a pea, Paw."

"Ha'e ye gotten a pistol?"

"Ay. It's wee Joseph's. He wis gaun to gi'e me it fur the book, but noo I jist got the len' o' 't. I'm vexed I hurtit ye."

"Weel, weel, we'll say nae mair aboot that, Macgreegor, but ye mauna fire at folk like thon again. Mind that, or ye'll maybe get the nick."

"I'll never dae't again, Paw."

"A' richt, ma mannie. But ye best rin ower to wee Joseph an' gi'e him back his pistol."

"But he'll no' ha'e read the book yet," objected Macgregor.

"Never heed. Let him keep the book till he's read it; but gi'e him back his pistol."

John spoke firmly, and Macgregor felt that he must obey.

"I'll gang up to the hoose," said his father, who had great difficulty in keeping his secret.

Ten minutes later Macgregor, having dutifully accomplished his errand, reached home to find his father firing peas at a mustard tin on the mantelpiece, and his mother applauding or commiserating the sportsman.

John immediately placed the weapon in the boy's hands. "There, ma mannie," he said, "there a pistol fur ye!"

Macgregor looked at his mother.

She nodded. "Be awfu' carefu' noo, dearie," she said.

Somehow the youngster was touched. "I'm no' heedin' aboot it, Maw! I'm no' awfu' heedin' aboot it!" he cried, and ran to her arms.

. . . .

Later on he pointed out that it wasn't quite such a good one as wee Joseph's.

XX

"FOR GRANPAW PURDIE"

"D'ye ken, John, that fayther an' mither'll ha'e been mairrit fifty year on the seventh o' Mairch?" said Mrs Robinson one January evening as, having put her little daughter to bed, she joined her husband at the kitchen fire and prepared to do some sewing.

"Is that a fac'?" exclaimed Mr Robinson, laying aside his evening paper. "I didna think they wis that auld."

"They're no' that auld, man! Ma fayther wis jist twinty-wan, and ma mither wis nineteen when they got mairrit."

"It's you bein' the youngest that confuses me, wumman. But it's a great thing to be mairrit fifty year. Dod, is it! I suppose they'll be haudin' a dimond jubilee."

"A golden waddin' ye mean, John. I've nae doot they wull. An' I wis thinkin' it wud be nice if we gi'ed them a bit present."

"'Deed, ay!" her husband agreed heartily.

"Paw," exclaimed Macgregor, looking up from his reading and spelling book, which he was supposed to be studying diligently, "is Granpaw Purdie gaun to get mairrit again?"

"Na, na. He an' yer Granmaw's gaun to haud their golden waddin'—jist like haudin' Ne'erday, ye ken—because they've been mairrit fur fifty year."

"I wudna like to be mairrit fur fifty year, Paw. Wull there be a pairty?"

"Haud yer tongue, laddie," interposed his mother. "Attend to yer lessons."

"I ken them, Maw."

"Are ye shair? Whit aboot yer spellin'?"

"I ken it."

"An' the meanin's o' a' the big words? Are ye shair ye ken them a'?"

"Ay, Maw."

"Aweel, let's see the book, an' I'll hear ye twa-three meanin's. . . . H'm! Whit's the meanin' o' the word *corporation*?"

"That's no' in the lesson."

"But it's markit."

"Ay, but that wis yesterday's. The morn's lesson's on the ither page."

"But ye sud ken the meanin' of *corporation*, if it wis in yer lesson yesterday."

"I kent it, but—but I furget."

Lizzie shook her head. "I doot, I doot ye're vera careless."

"I dinna see the use o' big words like thur," said the boy rebelliously. "They're jist daft!"

"Haud yer tongue, an' tell me the meanin' o' the word *temperate*."

"It means angry—ragin'."

"Na, na. Whit's the meanin' o' the word *current*?"

"It's a kin' o' frit, Maw," he replied hopefully.

"If ye had lukit at yer lesson, ye wudna ha'e said that, Macgreegor. Can ye tell me the meanin' o' the word *halibut*?"

"It's a thing fur playin' tunes on."

"Tits, laddie! It's a fish."

"It's no' a fish in the Bible, fur we had it in wur Bible lesson on Monday, an' it wis a thing fur playin' on."

"Ach, ye mean *sackbut*—whitever that means," said Mrs Robinson. "Na, na. I doot ye dinna ken yer meanin's. But I'll gi'e ye yin mair. Whit's the meanin' o' the word *contemplate*?"

"It means to be ashamed," replied Macgregor after considerable reflection.

"It disna! But ye micht weel be ashamed o' yersel', Macgreegor! Tak' yer book, an' dinna lift yer een frae it fur hauf an 'oor, an' then I'll hear ye yer meanin's again, an' yer spellin' furbye."

Taking the book from his mother, Macgregor returned unwillingly to his seat, while his father, who was glad when the little examination was over, jocularly observed:

"Never heed, ma mannie. Ye'll dae a' richt next time! There's some o' yer words wud puzzle me. Eh, Lizzie?"

"Ye needna confess yer eegnorance afore the wean, onywey," muttered Lizzie, with a touch of sharpness. "That's no' the wey to gar him strive wi' his lessons."

John accepted the reproof in silence, and presently changed the subject by inquiring:

"Whit wis ye thinkin' o' daein' aboot the golden jubilee —I mean the waddin', Lizzie?"

"Paw, is a julibee the same as a pairty?" asked Macgregor.

"Macgregor," said his mother, "I tell't ye to learn yer meanin's."

"But I want to ken the meanin' o' *julibee*, Maw."

"Weel, I'll maybe tell ye the meanin' o' the word *jubilee* —no' *julibee*—when ye can say yer lesson fur the morn." Mrs Robinson turned once more to her husband. "I wis thinkin', John," she said softly, "it wud be a rale nice thing to gi'e mither a wee gold brooch—if ye think we can afford it. I've nae doot we wud get yin aboot——"

"Oh, I think we'll manage that, wumman. I suppose yer brither Rubbert an' his guidwife'll be gi'ein' somethin' very graun'."

"Vera likely. Mistress Purdie wis sayin' it wis an occasion when somethin' gorgeous wis the correc' thing. But you an' me, John, canna keep up wi' her an' Rubbert."

"An' we're no' gaun to try it. We'll jist dae wur best, Lizzie, an' gi'e yer mither as guid a present as——"

"Paw, I want to gi'e Granpaw Purdie a present," cried Macgregor, and dropped his book with a smack on the floor.

"Is that no' nice o' the wean!" John exclaimed, gazing at his wife in admiration.

"'Deed, ay," she assented, trying not to look as gratified as she felt. "But pick up yer book an' gang on wi' yer lesson, dearie, an' then we'll think aboot yer present fur yer Granpaw."

"Is the julibee shin, Maw?" he inquired, as he secured his book.

"No' fur sax weeks. But gang on wi' yer lesson, like a guid laddie."

"But wull I be there, Maw?"

"We'll see, we'll see."

"'Deed, ye'll be there, Macgreegor," cried his father. "But dae as yer Maw bids ye the noo," he added, catching a look from Lizzie.

"But whit'll I gi'e to Granpaw fur his julibee?"

His mother repressed her impatience and said quietly: "Weel, dearie, yer Paw an' me'll see aboot that; an' ye better begin to save yer pennies, an' we'll add them to wur ain, an' buy somethin' fine fur yer Granpaw. Ye see? Noo try an' learn yer——"

"But I want to gi'e him a present masel'," the youngster objected.

"I doot ye'll no' ha'e enough pennies in time, Macgreegor."

"Ay, I wull."

"Let him try, Lizzie," interposed John.

"Wull ye promise no' to gi'e him mair nor his usual Setturday penny, John?" she asked quickly.

"A'richt, wumman," he stammered, reddening.

"Aweel," said his wife, with the faintest suspicion of a smile, "Macgreegor can try. Ye've sax weeks, Macgreegor, to save up fur yer Granpaw's present, so ye maun be carefu' wi' yer pennies, an' no' be spendin' them as shin's ye get them on trash."

"I'll be awfu' carefu', Maw," said her son in the first flush of a generous impulse. "But I wunner whit I'll buy fur Granpaw. I wud like to buy a——"

"Noo that'll dae," his mother interrupted firmly. "It's near time fur yer bed, an' if ye canna say yer lesson when the time's up, ye'll ha'e to rise early the morn's mornin', fur I'm no' gaun to ha'e ye sittin' at the fit o' the cless a' the year roon'."

"I wudna ha'e been fit the day, if Wullie Thomson hadna been absent. It wis his turn to be fit. If he disna be fit the morn, I'll bash him!"

"If ye say anither word, Macgreegor, I'll sen' ye to bed this vera meenit, an' I'll mak' ye rise at sax. You an' Wullie micht think shame o' yersel's! I'm thinkin' Wullie's maybe no' the richt companion fur ye, an' if ye dinna dae better shin I'll no' let ye gang wi' him. Mind that!"

"Wullie's faur nicer nor ony o' the ither laddies, an'——"

"'Sh!"

The interjection warned Macgregor that further conversation on his part would not be tolerated, and after a glance at his father, who, however, appeared to be deeply immersed in the contents of the evening paper, he bent over his lesson-book and endeavoured to master, for the time being at least, the spellings and meanings of two short columns of more or less long words.

. . . .

The weeks slipped away, and so, alas! did Macgregor's pennies. Perhaps it was more habit than actual selfishness that proved too strong for the boy. The coin he received immediately after dinner each Saturday he at first mentally dedicated to the purchase of a gift for Grandfather Purdie, but somehow before the afternoon was over it lay in the till of Mrs Juby's sweet-shop, while Macgregor and his chum Willie Thomson consumed the proceeds. It had, indeed, occurred to the careful Lizzie to offer herself as banker for the time being, but her husband had said, "Let him try whit he can save hissel'," and she had agreed, though not too hopefully.

So it came to pass that a couple of days before the old folks' "julibee," as he persisted in terming it, Macgregor's total assets were a bankrupt pocket, a worrying conscience, and a still earnest desire to show his affection for "Granpaw" with something tangible.

But love will find a way.

And on the evening before the happy anniversary he entered the home kitchen with his desire, if not his conscience, abundantly satisfied.

His parents were engaged in examining and admiring the brooch which Lizzie had chosen for her mother, and the pipe John had selected for his father-in-law, and both were secretly wondering if aught had come of their son's generous resolve.

"Here, Macgreegor!" cried John. "Come awa' an' tell us whit ye think o' thur."

"Canny noo, dearie, an' dinna drap the pipe," said Lizzie warningly.

"It's awfu' like the yin Granpaw broke at Rothesay last year," observed Macgregor. "I gi'ed him yin that whustled like a birdie, but I never heard him playin' on it. I wis aye to learn him. Maybe he hadna enough breith fur to play on it."

"It micht gar him hoast, ye ken," said Lizzie, "an' ye wudna like that." She and John were highly gratified to think that the new pipe might replace Mr Purdie's old and much-mourned favourite.

"An' hoo dae ye like the brooch, ma mannie?" John inquired, laying an arm about the boy's shoulders.

"It's gey wee," Macgregor replied after a brief inspection.

"Ay, but ye see it's gold—rale gold," his mother informed him. "Gold's awfu' dear, ye ken."

"Ay, it's gey dear. I bocht a—a—gaird fur Granpaw," he blurted out suddenly.

"A whit?" exclaimed Lizzie.

"A watch-gaird," said her son, very red and fumbling in his breast pocket. "It's a rale fine yin."

"Dod, but the wean's got a present fur his Granpaw!" cried John, delighted.

Macgregor at last produced a crumpled packet, and with trembling fingers unfolded it, laying bare a glittering and massive watch-chain.

K

"Mercy on us!" Lizzie ejaculated, as her husband took it in his hands.

"It's gold, Paw!" said the youngster in a hoarse whisper, his excitement getting the better of his conscience.

"Ay, nae doot it's gold, Macgreegor," said his father, with a discreet wink to Mrs Robinson.

"Whit did ye pey for this, laddie?" she asked, taking it from her husband's hand.

"Thruppence."

"'Deed, ye've done weel, ma mannie!" said John proudly.

Whereupon the young conscience gave a nasty twinge.

"Ay, ye've done rale weel, dearie," added his mother, pretending to feast her eyes on the clumsy imitation. "Ye've done rale weel," she repeated softly.

Macgregor tried to speak, but could not. His readiness and jauntiness deserted him.

One of John's hands stole to the pocket where he kept his purse. "Lizzie?" he muttered inquiringly.

She frowned for a moment; then she nodded. "I'm ower weel pleased to try to prevent ye, John," she whispered.

"Macgreegor," said his father. "Yer Maw an' me's rale pleased wi' ye fur savin' yer money to buy yer Granpaw a present. I cudna ha'e done it masel' when I wis a laddie like you. An' here a saxpence fur ye."

The boy took the gift, but the words "Thenk ye, Paw," would not pass his lips.

And all of a sudden the sixpence fell from his fingers, and rolled across the floor, and Macgregor dropped on his father's breast sobbing very bitterly.

It was some time ere the incoherent confession conveyed any meaning to the alarmed parents.

"But," said his mother at last, "if ye spent a' yer Setturday pennies, whaur got ye the money to buy the watch-gaird? Come awa', Macgreegor. Jist tell yer Paw an' me a' aboot it."

"P—Peter, Maw," mumbled the penitent.

"Wha?" asked John gently.

"P—patient Peter; or the Drunkard's Son. Oh! Oh!"

"Whit dis he mean?" the parents cried together. Then the truth dawned on Lizzie.

"Is't the nice book ye got frae yer Aunt Purdie on yer birthday?" she inquired in a shocked voice.

"Ay. . . . But it wisna a nice book."

"But hoo did ye get the money?" asked John, signing to his wife to keep silent. "Did ye sell the book?"

"N—na. I gi'ed it til wee Joseph, an'—an' he gi'ed me his p—pistol."

"But ye've a pistol o' yer ain, Macgreegor."

"Ay. But I gi'ed wee Joseph's pistol til Wullie Thomson, an' he gi'ed me a—a—a knife an' a big bew pincil; an' I gi'ed the knife til Geordie Scott fur tippence an' the pincil til Jimsie M'Faurlan fur a penny, an' then I—I bocht the gaird, an'—an' it wasna a nice book onywey." And here Macgregor broke down.

"Lizzie," whispered John awkwardly, "wull ye no' tak' him aside ye? Aw, Lizzie!"

"Come ower aside me, laddie," she said after a brief hesitation. . . . "Whit am I to say to ye?" she asked, wiping his eyes. "Ye ken it wisna the richt thing to dae . . . dearie. Wis it, noo?"

"N—naw. But—but I—I cudna help it, Maw."

"Weel, this is whit ye've got to dae. I'll get anither book fur wee Joseph, an' ye'll get yer ain yin back, an' ye'll gi'e me a ha'penny every Setturday till the new yin's peyed fur. Wull ye dae that?"

"Ay, Maw. But—but——"

"He's wantin' ye to say ye furgi'e him, Lizzie," said John. "Is that no' it, Macgreegor?"

The youngster nodded and hid his face on his sleeve.

His mother took him in her arms.

When he had gone to bed comforted, she picked up the sixpence that had lain neglected on the floor, remarking to her husband: "I'm gaun to keep it, John."

"D'ye think it's a vera lucky yin, wife?" he asked anxiously.

"I'm thinkin' it is," said Lizzie, who as a rule was not given to sentiment.

XXI

FELLOW-TRAVELLERS

"But I cud gang to Rothesay ma lane, Maw," said Macgregor eagerly. "I'm no' feart."

"I've nae doot ye wud gang to Jericho yer lane, if ye got the chance," his mother returned.

"Whaur's that?"

The boy's father laughed. "I hope ye ken, Lizzie."

Lizzie ignored him.

"If ye dinna like to gang wi' yer Aunt Purdie, Macgregor," she said firmly, "ye'll jist ha'e to bide at hame."

"Aunt Purdie's an auld——"

"Haud yer tongue!"

"Whit wey can Paw no' gang wi' me?" asked Macgregor, looking from one parent to the other.

Mr Robinson was about to reply, but his wife was before him.

"I've tell't ye hauf-a-dizzen o' times yer Paw has got to be at the new works till eleeven o'clock on Setturday, an' back again at five o'clock on Monday mornin'. It wis vera kind o' yer Aunt Purdie to offer to tak' ye when she kent yer Paw cudna gang."

"She didna offer to tak' me. Granpaw Purdie said she *wis* to tak' me. She didna *want* to tak' me—an' I dinna want to be tooken."

"Weel, weel; ye'll jist bide at hame."

"But I want to gang to Rothesay to see ma Granpaw Purdie. He likes me to gang to see him," said Macgregor.

His father, who was smilingly allowing his daughter to

exercise her small fingers on his hair, said mildly: "Weel, ma mannie, I think ye better jist mak' up yer mind to gang wi' yer Aunt Purdie. She's maybe no' jist——"

"John!" cried Lizzie warningly.

"Aweel, Macgreegor, as I wis gaun to say, ye maun try to be discreet aboot whit ye say aboot yer Aunt Purdie," Mr Robinson resumed. "She's maybe no'—I mean to say I'm sair vexed I canna gang wi' ye as I expectit, but ye ken it's a big job removin' to new works, an' I think ye're better to gang wi' yer Aunt Purdie nor no' gang ava. She'll be stoppin' in her ain hoose at Rothesay, so ye needna be feart——"

"I'm no feart fur her, Paw. She's feart fur me!"

John stifled a guffaw. "Weel, ma mannie," he went on soberly, "ye'll jist gang wi' her, an'—an' be a guid laddie, an' no' play ony pranks on the boat. Eh?"

There being no help for it, Macgregor at last agreed to travel to Rothesay in the company of Mrs Purdie, and the next day found the twain at St Enoch Station, with but little enough time in which to catch the train.

"I kent we wud be late," panted the boy, as he lugged along the old black bag wherein the careful Lizzie had packed articles which seemed quite unnecessary to her son. "I kent we wud be late," he repeated.

Aunt Purdie vouchsafed no reply, possibly because she had exhausted most of her breath on a porter who, after warning her repeatedly, had gently charged her in the rear with a luggage-laden barrow.

They clambered into a compartment just as the guard blew his whistle. There was one corner seat vacant, and into it sank Mrs Purdie.

Macgregor stood by the door.

"Sit down, Macgregor," commanded his aunt, indicating with a dignified finger the place at her side.

"I want to see oot," said Macgregor, unintentionally treading on one of his relative's cloth boots.

"Siddoon this meenit!" cried Mrs Purdie angrily, "or I'll no' tak' ye wi' me."

"Ye canna help it; the train's stairtit," her nephew retorted. "I didna mean to tramp on yer fit," he added, remembering the advice of his parents. "Wis it a corn?"

"Siddoon!" said Mrs Purdie in an awful whisper.

"But I canna see onythin' when I'm sittin' doon," said Macgregor, obeying with great reluctance.

An elderly man on the other side of the compartment smiled pleasantly and offered the boy his corner seat, observing to Mrs Purdie that young people liked to see what was passing.

Macgregor rose eagerly, but his aunt gripped his arm and forced him back upon the seat.

"Thank you," she said majestically to the elderly man, "but kindly reserve your seat for yoursel'."

Whereupon the elderly man looked rather astonished and retired behind his paper.

At the affront Macgregor got red in the face, and his eyes may have grown a little moist; but he said nothing.

Presently Mrs Purdie opened a small handbag, made from the skin of a German crocodile and richly ornamented with the gold of Abyssinia, and took out a handkerchief redolent of "Love's Young Dream" perfume and a current copy of *Our Happy Home*. She sniffed into the handkerchief, replaced it in the bag, and opened the periodical.

Macgregor looked over her arm at the page, but portraits of and paragraphs about titled or wealthy people did not interest him. He searched in his pockets and found a tiny cake of india-rubber. This he slipped into his mouth and chewed till the train stopped at Paisley, when a desire for conversation came upon him.

"Are we gaun in a boat wi' a rid funnel, Aunt Purdie?" he inquired.

"I have no ideer. Don't speak with your mouth full," his aunt replied. "What are you eatin'?"

"It's jist a wee bit injia-rubber," said Macgregor. "The best wey to clean injia-rubber's to sook it."

"Feech!" exclaimed Mrs Purdie, forgetting, as she did

when excited, her more refined manner of speech. "Pit it awa' at once."

"I like chowin' it," he returned. "Can I get staunin' at the winda noo?"

"No, you cannot. Sit still and behave!"

"Whit wey can I no'?"

Mrs Purdie turned a page without replying.

"Here the man fur the tickets," Macgregor remarked.

"They don't take them here," snapped Mrs Purdie.

"Tickets, please!" said the collector, opening the door.

"I tell't ye!" Macgregor said triumphantly.

Mrs Purdie eyed the collector as if she could have bitten him.

"I tell't ye!" said Macgregor again, when the man had gone.

"Haud yer tongue!" muttered Mrs Purdie.

Macgregor glanced at the other passengers with a slight smile, perhaps of pity for his relative.

Five minutes later he withdrew the india-rubber from his mouth, regarded it with satisfaction—it was certainly much cleaner-looking than it had been prior to its insertion —dried it on his stocking, and returned it to his pocket.

He nudged his aunt gently, and inquired: "Can I get staunin' at the winda noo?"

"Certainly not!" said Mrs Purdie. "And you needna ask again. Sit still and behave!"

"I'm wearyin'," he whispered.

"Well, behave yourself, and you'll soon be there."

"We're no' hauf roads yet."

Mrs Purdie resumed reading about the domestic virtues of a millionaire marchioness, and Macgregor once more searched his pockets for some distraction. He was, however, wearing his good clothes, and his mother had taken care that the miscellaneous collection of treasures and curios should not be transferred from his everyday garments. The india-rubber had been a happy exception.

"I wud like to luk at the pipe," he said at last. He had purchased a fancy clay pipe as a present for his grandfather, and his mother had recommended that, for its safety, his aunt should carry it in her handbag. This had been done, though not with the boy's approval.

Mrs Purdie, lost in admiration of the marchioness who, for the benefit of the public, had been photographed cuddling a baby, murmured: "Never heed the pipe the noo. It's safest whaur it is."

"But I want to see it, please," said Macgregor politely, remembering once more his mother's instructions.

"Ye'll get it afterwards. Sit still and behave."

"Wull I get it in five meenits?"

"We'll see."

"Wull I get it when we're on the boat?"

"Maybe. Sit still and behave," said Mrs Purdie absently.

"I'm sittin' still, an' I'm behavin'," said Macgregor, to the delight of several of the passengers. "Gi'e's ma pipe!"

Mrs Purdie paid no attention. The marchioness had been known to bath her baby with her own hands!

"Gi'e's ma pipe!" said Macgregor again, the least thing threateningly.

"That's not the way to ask for it," said his aunt coldly.

"If ye please."

Mrs Purdie, with a haughty stare round the compartment, laid down *Our Happy Home*, and in a leisurely fashion opened her bag. She took out her handkerchief, sniffed into its scented folds, and returned it to its place. As she did so the expression of her countenance changed. She put her hand into the bag, fumbled for a few seconds, and withdrew it.

"Ye'll get yer pipe later on," she said, and shut the bag with a snap.

"But I want it the noo."

"Sit still and behave," said Mrs Purdie, and returned to the marchioness. But the doings of the marchioness had lost their charm.

The pipe was not in her bag! She must have dropped it

when she was buying the tickets, or maybe when she was purchasing *Our Happy Home*. It was more than enough to know that it had gone. It was a wretched predicament in which to find herself. Whatever might happen afterwards, she must at all costs keep the loss from her nephew until Rothesay was reached.

"Wull I get it on the boat?" persisted the boy.

"Sit still and behave." She could think of nothing else to say.

It would be difficult to state which of the relatives found the remainder of the journey the more trying, but as the train slowed into Prince's Pier Mrs Purdie was the first to make for the door, which was at the far end of the compartment.

Macgregor was about to follow, when his arm was caught, and something was slipped into his free hand, while the elderly man who had offered to give up his corner whispered:

"She's not your mother, is she?"

"Naw," said the boy quickly. "Whaur did ye——"

"It's your pipe," interrupted the man. "She dropped it. Put it in your pocket. She thinks she has lost it. Don't tell her you've got it till you've had some fun out of her. Eh?"

And he pushed the boy to the door, chuckling as he did so.

Macgregor followed his aunt, grinning and feeling the pipe in his pocket. The pipe had been too well wrapped in paper to have suffered injury from a mere fall.

Mrs Purdie bustled on board the steamer, and presently she and her nephew had deposited their little luggage in a suitable corner. A rather keen wind was blowing.

"We best retire to the saloon, Macgregor," said the aunt in a pleasanter tone than she had so far used.

"I want to see the ingynes," said the nephew.

"You'll see the ingynes another time."

"I want to see them noo."

Mrs Purdie went back to her high-handed methods.

She grabbed her nephew by the arm, saying: "Come away to the saloon this meenit, and sit still and behave!"

"Weel, gi'e's ma pipe," said Macgregor.

Mrs Purdie hesitated. "If I let you see the ingynes the now, will you promise to come to the saloon afterwards?"

"Ay—if ye'll gi'e's ma pipe."

They watched the engines till the hot air and the odour of oil well-nigh overcame Mrs Purdie.

She moved in the direction of the saloon.

"We'll gang to the neb o' the boat noo," said her nephew.

"That we will not," she retorted promptly. "I'm not wantin' to get my death of cold."

"I can gang masel," said Macgregor.

"I'll not permit it. You'll fall in the sea."

"Nae fears!"

"Ye've jist got to come to the saloon this meenit!"

"Gi'e's ma pipe, then," was the reply.

They went together to the bow of the steamer, where Mrs Purdie's new bonnet, trimmed with two apricots and one dozen cherries, was nearly torn from her head by the blast.

"Ye wee rascal!" she cried, fuming, "if ye dinna come to the saloon noo, I'll tell yer Maw, so I will!"

"But I'm no' wantin' to gang to the saloon. I'm gaun to hear the baun' playin'. Thonder it is, ahint the funnel. The sea's gettin' lumpy. D'ye feel it?"

Mrs Purdie did feel it. She was a bad sailor, and the merest swell upset her.

"It's ower cauld on the deck," she said, after three minutes beside the band. "Come doon to the saloon, and sit still and behave," she added, but with little spirit in her words.

"Wull ye gi'e's ma pipe?"

Mrs Purdie was beaten. "If I leave ye here," she said unwillingly, "will ye promise no' to gang near the side?"

"Ay," said Macgregor readily. "Dinna be feart fur me. I ken whit I'm daein'. Jist you gang doon to the saloon, an' I'll see ye at Rothesay."

She turned away, and Macgregor proceeded to divert himself. Never—even in his father's charge—had he enjoyed such freedom on board a steamer. Within the space of five minutes he was on the best of terms with himself and the whole world, but it was not until the hour's passage was almost over that it occurred to him to have a peep at his aunt. As he went in the direction of the saloon he wondered what his aunt would say when she beheld him presenting his grandfather with the pipe—which little ceremony he had decided should take place on Rothesay quay. He was not quite sure whether he should tell his grandfather of the pipe's adventure.

He halted at the saloon entrance and peeped in. Few passengers were there, and his aunt had a sofa to herself. She was half sitting, half reclining, and was holding her handkerchief to her face, almost covering it.

Macgregor stared in wonder, not unmixed with alarm. What was wrong with her? Then all at once he understood. It was the loss of the pipe. Aunt Purdie was afraid; perhaps she was even sorry. Macgregor realized that at once. Well, it served her right! He would go and have another look at the engines. So he went to the engine-room, but somehow the engines were not quite so interesting as they had been an hour earlier.

He returned to the saloon entrance and peeped in again. She was still there, just as before. Macgregor did not feel exactly sorry, but he felt he ought to say or do something. On tiptoe he entered the saloon and stood beside her. She did not move.

His eye fell upon *Our Happy Home* and the handbag lying on the seat—open. On a sudden impulse he drew the little parcel from his pocket and laid it quietly in the bag. Then he stole away out of the saloon.

.   .   .   .

After the greetings on Rothesay quay Aunt Purdie hurried away, leaving old Mr Purdie and Macgregor to walk home leisurely.

"It wis a peety yer Aunt turned seeck on the boat," Mr Purdie remarked.

"She wisna seeck," said Macgregor, fingering the little parcel in his pocket. His aunt had given him the pipe without a word just before leaving the steamer. Her annoyance at her own carelessness rendered her dumb.

"I thocht I heard her say she wis," said the old man.

Macgregor knew better. He said nothing, but he knew that Aunt Purdie, bad as she was, had a conscience somewhere.

XXII

SHIPS THAT PASS

THE small boy in the trim sailor suit, broad-brimmed straw hat with "H.M.S. *Valiant*" in gold letters on the dark blue ribbon, spotless white collar with gold anchors at the corners, and fine shoes and stockings, stood helplessly on the sunlit shore, and with misty eyes gazed hopelessly at his toy yacht drifting out to sea.

"Whit wey dae ye no' wade in efter yer boat?" demanded Macgregor, who for half-an-hour had been envying the owner his pretty craft from a little distance, and who now approached the disconsolate youngster.

"Gaun! Tak' aff yer shoes an' stockin's quick, or ye'll loss yer boat," said Macgregor excitedly. "Gaun! Wade!" he repeated. "Are ye feart?"

"Mamma said I wasn't to wade," said the alleged member of the crew of "H.M.S. *Valiant*."

"Whit wey?"

"She said it was too cold." He gave a sniff of despair as his eyes turned to his toy.

"Ach! it's no' that cauld. I'll wade fur yer boat."

"Oh!" It was all he could say, but he looked with gratitude at Macgregor, who was already unlacing one of his stout boots.

A minute later Macgregor had rolled up his breeches, and, checking an exclamation at the first contact with the water, was wading gingerly after the model yacht.

"It's awfu' warm," he declared with a shiver.

"Don't get your trousers wet," said the other.

"Nae fears!" returned Macgregor, stepping into a small depression and soaking several inches of his nether garments. "I'm no' heedin', onywey," he said bravely.

"You can't get it. It's too deep," cried the anxious one on the shore. "Oh, my!"

The exclamation was caused by Macgregor taking a plunge forward, soaking his clothes still further, but grabbing successfully at the boat. Then he turned and waded cautiously to the shore, and presented the owner with his almost lost property, remarking: "There yer boat. Whit wey did ye no' keep a grup o' the string?"

The other clasped his treasure and gazed with speechless thankfulness at the deliverer.

"It's a daft-like thing to be sailin' a boat if ye dinna wade," observed Macgregor, sitting down on a rock and proceeding to dry his feet and legs with his bonnet. Suddenly he desisted from the operation, as if struck by an idea, and getting up again said easily: "I'll help ye to sail yer boat, if ye like."

The other looked doubtful for a moment, for Macgregor's previous remark had offended him somewhat.

"Come on," said Macgregor with increasing eagerness. "You can be the captain, an' I'll be the sailor."

Evidently overcome by the flattering proposal, the owner of the yacht nodded and allowed the proposer to take the craft from his hands.

"My! It's an unco fine boat!" Macgregor observed admiringly. "Whaur got ye it?"

"Uncle William gave me it," replied the other, beginning to find his tongue, "and it's called the *Britannia*."

"It's no' an awfu' nice name, but it's a fine boat. I wisht I had as fine a boat. . . . Whit's yer name?" he inquired, wading into the water. "Mines is Macgreegor Robison."

"Charlie Fortune."

"That's a queer-like name. Whaur d'ye come frae?"
Charlie looked puzzled.

"D'ye come frae Glesca? Eh?"

"Yes."

"I never seen ye afore. Whaur d'ye bide in Glesca?"

"Kelvinside. Royal Gardens, Kelvinside."

"Aw, ye'll be gentry," said Macgregor scornfully.

"I don't know," said Charlie. "Are you—gentry?"

"Nae fears! I wudna be gentry for onythin'!"

Charlie did not quite understand. Presently he asked
shyly: "Has your mamma got a house at Rothesay?"

"Naw. But Granpaw Purdie's got a hoose, an' I'm
bidin' wi' him. Hoo lang are ye bidin' in Rothesay?"

"Three months."

"My! I wisht I wis you! I'm gaun hame next week. . . .
But I'll be back again shin. Granpaw Purdie likes when
I'm bidin' wi' him. Thon's him ower thonder." And
Macgregor indicated the distant figure of the old man,
who sat on a boulder reading a morning paper.

Mr Purdie reminded Charlie of an old gardener
occasionally employed by his wealthy father, but he offered
no remark, and Macgregor placed the boat in the water,
crying out with delight as her sails caught a mild breeze.

"Gang ower to thon rock," Macgregor commanded,
forgetting in his excitement that, being the sailor, it was
not his place to give orders, "an' I'll gar the boat sail to ye."

Charlie obediently made for a spur of rock that entered
the water a few yards, and waited there patiently while his
new acquaintance managed the yacht, not perhaps very
skilfully, but entirely to his own satisfaction.

"I'm daein' fine, am I no'?" exclaimed Macgregor, as
he approached the captain, who had soaked his nice brown
shoes in a shallow pool and was now crouching on a slippery
rock, fearful lest his mother should come down to the shore
and catch him.

"I'm daein' fine, am I no'?" repeated Macgregor.

"Yes," returned Charlie rather dejectedly.

"Weel, I'll tak' the boat ower thonder an' sail it back to ye again."

"I wish I could sail the boat, too," said Charlie.

"But ye canna sail it if ye canna get takin' yer bare feet. But never heed. Captains never tak' their bare feet," said Macgregor, wading off with the yacht.

He enjoyed himself tremendously for nearly an hour, at the end of which period Charlie announced timidly that it was time for him to go home.

"Wull ye be here in the efternune?" inquired Macgregor, leaving the water on bluish feet and relinquishing the *Britannia* with obvious regret.

"No, I'm going to drive with mamma."

"Are ye gaun in the bus? Granpaw whiles tak's me fur a ride to——"

"Mamma has a carriage," said Charlie.

"I thocht ye wis gentry," said Macgregor, with a pitying gaze at Charlie. There was a pause, and then his eyes turned again to the yacht. "Wull ye be here the morn?"

"I don't know," said Charlie, who wasn't sure that he liked Macgregor's manner of speech, but who still felt grateful to him and was also impressed by his sturdiness.

"Ye micht try an' come. An' tell yer maw ye want to tak' yer bare feet, an' we'll baith be sailors. Eh?"

"I'll try. Thank you for—for saving my boat."

"Aw, never heed that. Jist try an' come the morn, an' I'll come early an' build a pier fur the boat."

"I'll try," said Charlie once more; and with a smile on his small, delicate face he hurried up the beach.

Macgregor warmed his legs on the sunny shingle and got into his boots and stockings; then rejoined his grandfather, hoping the old man would not notice the damp condition of his breeches.

Mr Purdie laid down his paper and smilingly looked at his grandson over his spectacles.

"I see ye've been makin' a new freen', Macgreegor. Whit laddie wis thon?"

"Chairlie—I furget his ither name. He lost his boat, an' I tuk ma bare feet an' gaed in an' got it fur him."

Mr Purdie beamed with pride, and patted the boy's shoulder. "'Deed, that wis rale kind o' ye, ma mannie. He wid be gled to get back his boat, an' he wud be unco obleeged to yersel' fur gettin' it. I'm thinkin' ye deserve a penny." And out came the old man's purse.

"Thenk ye, Granpaw. . . . An' then I sailed his boat fur him. He canna sail it hissel', fur his maw winna let him tak' his bare feet. She maun be an auld daftie!"

"Whisht, whisht!" said Mr Purdie reprovingly. "But whit like is Chairlie?"

"Och, he's gey peely-wally, an' I think he's gentry, but his boat's an awfu' fine yin."

"Whit gars ye think he's gentry?"

"He bides in Kelvinside, an' his maw rides in a cairriage, an' he speaks like Aunt Purdie when she's ha'ein' a pairty."

At the last reason Mr Purdie gave a half-suppressed chuckle. "Weel, weel, Macgreegor, ye're gettin' on. Ye're the yin to notice things."

"Ay; I'm gey fly, Granpaw," said Macgregor.

"But mind an' no' lead Chairlie intil ony mischief," Mr Purdie went on. "An' ye're no' to temp' him to tak' his bare feet if his mither disna want him to dae it. Noo it's time we wis gaun hame to wur dinner. Gi'e's yer haun', ma mannie."

Next day, when Macgregor had almost given up hope, and stood disconsolately eyeing the pier he had constructed as promised, Charlie arrived panting, with the *Britannia* in his arms.

"I thocht ye wisna comin'," said Macgregor.

"Mamma didn't want me to play on the shore to-day."

"Did ye rin awa' frae her the noo?"

"No. But Uncle William came in, and he asked her for me, and then she said I could go for half-an-hour. But I'm not to go wading."

"Are ye no'? I wudna like to be you," said Macgregor, dabbling his bare feet in the water. "Weel, ye can be the man on the pier. Some o' the stanes is a wee thing shoogly, but ye'll jist ha'e to luk whaur ye pit yer feet, Chairlie."

Charlie, after a little hesitation, walked gingerly down the narrow passage of loose stones which terminated with a large flat one, where he found a fairly sure foot-hold.

"That's it!" cried Macgregor, wading out from shore till the water was within half-an-inch of his clothing. "Ye're jist like a pier-man."

Charlie was so gratified that he nearly fell off his perch. Very cautiously he placed his model afloat, and the wind carried it out to sea, Macgregor moving along so as to intercept it.

Macgregor wanted to have the *Britannia* sail back to its owner, but the mystery of navigation was too much for him, so he carried it to Charlie, who set it off again.

After all, it wasn't such bad fun being a pier-man, and in about ten minutes the youngsters were as friendly as could be. And they spent a glorious hour and a quarter.

"Wull ye be here the morn?" asked Macgregor when his new chum said, rather fearfully, that he must depart.

"Yes." There was a flush on Charlie's face that ought to have done his mother good to see. "Yes," he repeated eagerly. "And I'll bring my other boat."

"My! Ha'e ye anither boat, Chairlie?"

Charlie nodded. "Not as big as the *Britannia*," he said. . . . He smiled shyly at his friend. "I—I'm going to give it to you, Macgreegor," he stammered, pronouncing the name as he had heard it from its owner.

"Ach, ye're jist sayin' that!" cried Macgregor, overcome with astonishment.

"Really and truly," said Charlie.

"Ye—ye're faur ower kind," whispered Macgregor, fairly at a loss for once in his little life.

Feeling and looking awkward and more awkward, Charlie took the liberty of touching Macgregor's arm.

"Please promise to take the boat," he murmured.

Macgregor fumbled in his pocket. "I'll gi'e ye ma penny," he said, producing it.

L

But Charlie drew back, and somehow Macgregor understood that he had done something stupid.

Charlie ran off, and Macgregor, gazing curiously after him, resumed his boots and stockings.

The day following was as wet as it can be on the West coast of Scotland and, in spite of Macgregor's open yearning for his new toy, his grandparents would not allow him out of doors.

"Maybe Chairlie'll be there wi' ma boat," he pleaded.

But Grandfather Purdie gently said: "It's no' vera likely"; and Grandmother Purdie remarked: "Ye wud jist get yer daith o' cauld, ma dearie."

But the morning after broke brilliantly—too brilliantly, perhaps, to last.

At ten o'clock Mr Purdie was sitting on his favourite rock, his pipe in his mouth, his specs on his nose, and his newspaper before him. "I wud like to come an' see yer freen' Chairlie," he had said, ere his grandson left him; "I like weans that's kind til ither weans." And Macgregor had promised to wave a signal when Charlie came with the boats. Mr Purdie had filled his pocket with sweets for the occasion.

Macgregor reached the appointed place, which seemed so familiar, although it was only his third visit, and, his friend not being in sight, proceeded to repair the pier, which several tides had disarranged.

He became so busy and so interested that he did not hear the sound of flying feet until they were close upon him. Then he rose from his stooping posture and beheld Charlie with a beautiful little boat in his arms.

"Here's your boat, Macgreegor," gasped Charlie.

"My!" cried Macgregor, taking it. "Oh, Chairlie, ye're awfu'——"

"Mamma said I wasn't to play with you any more, but—but I ran away, and——"

"Whit wey?"

Charlie shook his head. "I like you," he panted. "I never had another boy to—to play with.   I—I——"

"*Charlie, come here at once!*"

"Good-bye, Macgregor," said Charlie, and turning, ran some fifty yards to the elegantly dressed lady who had called him.

"She's gentry," said Macgregor to himself, but he did not hear her say crossly to Charlie:

"What do you mean by speaking to that horrid boy after I told you never to speak to him again?"

Macgregor, after waiting in the hope that Charlie would return, hastened toward his grandfather to exhibit his prize, but as he proceeded his pace slackened.

"Ye've got yer boat, Macgreegor!" the old man exclaimed. "Dod, but it's a bonny boat! It wis unco kind o' Chairlie to gi'e ye that. But whit wey did ye no' wave on me? Eh? Is Chairlie waitin' ower thonder?"

Macgregor laid his boat on the ground. "Chairlie ran awa'. He said his maw didna want him to play wi' me ony mair. . . . Granpaw, whit wey——"

"Whit's that ye're sayin', Macgreegor?"

"Chairlie said his maw didna want him to play wi' me ony mair. . . . I think she's gentry—she's an auld footer. . . . I like Chairlie."

"Ah!" exclaimed Mr Purdie suddenly. Then he uttered several words, wildly.

Macgregor gasped. Never before had he heard his grandfather use such words.

XXIII

MRS M'OSTRICH GIVES ANOTHER PARTY

"I've news fur ye the nicht, John," said Mrs Robinson, shortly after the family had gathered at the tea-table, one evening towards the end of the year.

"Weel, I hope it's guid news, fur if it's bad I'll ha'e ma ham an' eggs first," returned her husband pleasantly.

"Oh, it's no' whit ye wud ca' bad news."

"*I* ken whit it is," exclaimed Macgregor, grinning. "It's aboot Mistress M'Ostrich. She's gaun to ha'e a pairty, an' I'm gaun!"

"Haud yer tongue, laddie," said his mother, slightly annoyed. "An' dinna speak wi' yer mooth fu' o' breid."

"It's no' breid, Maw; it's toast. I like Mistress M'Ostrich."

His father, checking a laugh, inquired the date of the party.

"The morn's nicht," replied Mrs Robinson. "I wis gaun to tell ye, John, that——"

"It's to be a hot supper, Paw, because Mistress M'Ostrich's uncle's deid," Macgregor interrupted gleefully.

"Tits! Macgreegor! Can ye no' haud yer tongue when I tell ye? An' ye're jist as bad, John, to lauch like that at his stupit sayin's."

"Och, Lizzie, I canna help lauchin'. But gang on wi' yer story, an' Macgreegor'll keep quate," said John, shaking his head at his son in a mildly warning fashion.

"Weel," said Lizzie, somewhat mollified, "I'll jist tell ye a' aboot it. (Macgreegor, butter a piece breid fur yer wee sister.) Mistress M'Ostrich cam' to me the day to tell me——"

"She got the len' o' wur bew vazes, Paw, an' wur mauve tidy wi' the yella paurrit on it, an' wur——"

"Whisht, man!" whispered John. "Never heed him, Lizzie," he added to his wife. "Whit did Mistress M'Ostrich tell ye?"

"She tell't me she had gotten near a hunner pound left her by her uncle in Americy. She hasna seen him fur thirty year——"

"Her uncle's deid, Paw."

The parents wisely ignored the interruption, and Mrs Robinson continued:

"An' she wis unco surprised at him mindin' her, fur he didna approve o' her mairryin' M'Ostrich. (Whit wis it ye wis wantin', Jeannie, ma doo?) Did Macgreegor no' pit plenty butter on yer piece? Macgreegor, pit mair butter on yer wee sister's piece, an' dinna mak' sic a noise drinkin' yer tea!) But fur a' that, she wis gled to get the money."

"Dod, ay!" said John. "I cud dae wi' 't masel! But I thocht she micht be gettin' vazes an' tidies o' her ain wi' some of the siller."

"Ah, but ye see, John, she hasna gotten the money yet; an', furbye, she said she didna like to gang past her auld freen's that had obleeged her mony a time afore."

"'Deed, that's yin wey o' lukin' at it," her husband remarked, smiling.

"Puir buddy, when I think o' her man, I canna grudge her onythin'. Fancy her man gaun aff to his bed i' the kitchen every nicht afore nine o'clock, an' her hearin' him snorin' a' the time she's ha'ein' a pairty in the paurlour."

"She sudna ha'e mairrit a baker. If M'Ostrich has got to rise early, he maun gang to his bed early. But it's a peety he's sic a snorer. D'ye mind—ha! ha!—when Macgreegor thocht there wis a pig in Mistress M'Ostrich's kitchen?"

"I'm no' likely to furget that, John! I never wis mair affrontit in a' ma born days. I'm shair I hope Macgreegor'll behave hissel' the morn's nicht," sighed Lizzie. "An' I'm feart he'll be nane the better o' the hot supper."

"I'll no' affront ye, Maw," put in Macgregor.

"I'm shair he'll no' affront ye," said John, patting the boy's shoulder.

"Weel, weel, dearie," said Lizzie to her son, "I jist hope ye'll be carefu' whit ye say, an' carefu' whit ye eat, an' no' be impiddent to yer Aunt Purdie."

"Is ma Aunt Purdie to be at the pairty?" Macgregor inquired, his face clouding.

"Vera likely."

"I thocht Mistress M'Ostrich wudna be genteel enough fur Mistress Purdie," John observed.

"We'll see," returned his wife briefly, turning to replenish her little daughter's mug with milk.

"Paw," said Macgregor in a confidential whisper, "if

Aunt Purdie's at the pairty, you an' me'll no' sit aside her."

.   .   .   .

Mrs M'Ostrich's little parlour was decorated in so lavish and varied a fashion by the numerous ornaments borrowed from her guests that the dinginess of its walls and the shabbiness of its furniture were hardly noticeable. But whatever anyone might feel about her method of obtaining decorations, no one could deny that her hospitality was exceedingly generous. It was almost a craze of the elderly childless woman to give parties as frequently as she could scrape together sufficient cash for more or less light refreshments; and on this occasion, when money, or at any rate the prospect of it, was assured, she rejoiced in loading her table with good things, turning a deaf ear to her husband's cry of "awfu' wastry." Moreover she had purchased a black silk dress—her dream of at least thirty years—which, besides accentuating the spareness of her figure, was likely to gain her the envy of not a few of her acquaintances. Yet with what conscious pride did she receive her guests, trying to forget that half-an-hour earlier Mr M'Ostrich had retired to rest without a word of admiration or encouragement, and that he might begin to snore at any moment!

Mrs Purdie was the last to arrive, as became one whose husband was a successful merchant, and she came more with a view to impressing the more humble guests with her importance than with any intention of making herself agreeable. It was quite a shock to her to find another silk dress in the parlour. She greeted the Robinsons in the patronizing way which always irritated John and Lizzie into saying very plain things and behaving in their most unaffected manner.

"And how are you to-night, Macgregor?" she inquired, smiling sourly upon her nephew.

"Fine, thenk ye," he returned, trying to edge away.

"I didn't think a little boy like you would have been allowed to sich a late party," she observed, so disagreeably that John, overhearing her, clenched his fist involuntarily.